MW00850019

BETTER Hide

THE RUN AND HIDE DUET

ALINA MAY

Ebook ISBN: 979-8-9888758-5-7

Paperback ISBN: 979-8-9888758-4-0

Hardcover ISBN: 979-8-9888758-6-4

Book Cover Occult Goddess

Formatting by Occult Goddess

Illustrations by Lulybot

Editing by Deliciously Dark Editing

Page Edge Design (hardcover) Painted Wing's Publishing

This content only suitable for 18+

To those who have fantasized about being kidnapped by toxic, red flag men. This one's for you.

AUTHOR'S NOTE

So my nasty, dirty hoes are back for more, huh? Masochists, lol.

Please be warned this book is dark. There are triggering themes such as non consent, sexy waterboarding, mental torture, manipulation, and many more. The relationships in this book are abusive and manipulative and should not be mimicked in real life.

Non consent is never hot in real life.

Please also note that this story is not meant to be a sexual guide.

Cool. Now that the formalities are out of the way...you ready to escape into some sick, depraved shit? Me too. Let's go.

Better Run Recap

Mary Jo is living in mediocrity when she's kidnapped by Jayden and Cole. At first, Jayden took Jo to get revenge on his ex-girlfriend Sage, but he also quickly became obsessed with Jo.

Jayden and Cole play fucked up games with Jo, forcing her to realize she likes the dark side of sex. During her time with them, Jo learns that Jayden and Cole have been sexually abused by Jayden's step dad, Pat.

Jayden then kidnaps Sage and Jo discovers that Sage fucked Pat as well as sold drugs to Jayden's mom, causing her to pass away. Jayden kills Sage in front of Jo.

Jo has a miscarriage, forcing the men to take her to the hospital where she escapes. She stays hidden for six months in Texas when the boys find her, carve their initials into her arm, and take her with them.

This story starts immediately after Jayden and Cole find Jo.

1

Hate sex is the best sex you'll ever get in your life.

Jayden collapses next to me, and I lay panting after yet another orgasm, looking at the chalky ceiling. My mind is a fuzzy mess of endorphins and adrenaline.

Jayden and Cole took me. Again. All of the hate and resentment and fucking loneliness over the last six months has come roaring back. The feelings rush through my veins like boiling water.

I can't believe they found me. They found me and took me. Again.

The smell of sweat and spearmint fills the room, and a mix of adrenaline and heat rushes through me again. It makes my clit throb.

Cole heaves his body off the bed. I watch as his big form moves to the dresser, clicks on a small lamp, and grabs a pill bottle out of his bag. I can't help but stare at him while he moves. His muscles catch the shadows, and he looks more tan than I remember.

Cole brings the pill bottle and a water bottle back to me.

"Here." He shakes one out and hands it to me.

I blink and sit up. The pill looks tiny in his huge hand.

They're giving me pills again. I flashback to the drugged pancakes and can almost taste the bitter syrup. Oh fuck no, this isn't happening again.

Cole lifts an eyebrow. "Take it, Jo."

My throat tightens, and I glare at him.

Jayden sits up next to me. His arms look dark in the low light and are covered in tattoos. He lowers his head beside mine and whispers low into my ear, "I would take great pleasure in forcing that pill down your pretty little throat." Jayden's hand traces up my bare arm, whispering around the base of my neck, causing goosebumps to prickle along my skin. "Maybe wash it down with a bit of cum, hmmm? You cry such delicious little tears when you panic." His fingers brush the side of my neck.

I shiver.

Cole grabs my hand and forces the pill into my palm. He winks. "Remember. We don't have to drug you to do what we want with you."

I shoot a glare at him. "This can't keep happening."

"What can't?" Cole's blue eyes watch me as I fist the pill.

"Forcing me to do things. Not giving me a say."

"That's kind of our thing, little one," Cole laughs. "But it's a pain pill. For your arm."

I glance down at my arm, where they carved their initials into me. It's been throbbing like a bitch, but the pain has been in the back of my mind while they've fucked the shit out of me.

Cole looks sincere, but then again, he always looks sincere. I gaze at the pill in my hand. It does look just like the one he gave me at the cabin for pain, and my arm is hot with pain. Reluctantly, I pop the pill in my mouth. Cole watches my throat bob as I dry-swallow it.

Jayden stands, going to the bathroom. He's big. Bigger than I remember him being.

I snap my gaze to Cole. "This has to be a two-way street. You can't just order me around like a dog."

Cole leans back on the bed, puts his hands behind his head, and watches me with a feline grin. "I can't?" His earring glints in the low light.

"No!" Both anger and horniness wash through me. How dare he be so attractive? I'd rehearsed everything I'd wanted to say for months. Last time, they took my freedom, my voice, my body.

Not this time. At least, not like they did before.

Jayden comes back, shaking water out of his dark hair. He's still completely naked, muscled, and covered in dark tattoos, which makes my breath hitch.

I draw in a breath. "I want my phone."

Jayden barely glances at me. "No."

Heat rushes over me, and I whirl on Cole. He's watching me intently.

"You heard the boss man."

No. I won't let this happen again. I'm going to take some of my power back.

I dart to my feet, heading for the bag I brought from Rosemary's house. It's on the table, right next to Jayden's.

Faster than I can register, one of Jayden's hands is on my throat, and the other is behind my head. He slams me against the wall, pinning me there against his solid, naked body. He presses into me, his hand firmly caging my neck.

"Fuck you," I hiss, struggling against him. "You can't keep doing this to me."

"Want to tell me again what I can't do?" Jayden bites down on my ear—hard. I yelp.

"Because from here, it looks like I can do whatever the fuck I want. And there's nothing you can do to stop me." Jayden's voice is low and rumbly. He pulls back enough to fix his dark eyes on me.

There's a flash of anger, and his voice deepens. "Is this what he did to you?"

Jayden's hand tightens around my throat, and I cough, grabbing at his hand. I'm confused. "What?"

"The guy you hooked up with." Jayden's hand tightens more, and disgust fills his gaze.

My head gets light. Oh shit. The only guy I went on a date with? The one who didn't even make it past first base?

"I...didn't..." I claw at Jayden's hand, but he doesn't let me go. "We didn't do anything."

"I should mark all the places he touched. Remove his touch from your skin."

Darkness flickers in my vision, and my heart pounds in my ears. "Did he touch you here?"

My whole body is tingling. Jayden lets up just enough that I suck in a breath, and my skin washes in heat.

Jayden cups my pussy. "Did. He. Touch. You. Here?"

My eyes move slowly. It's like I'm dreaming and trying to get my body to react. "No."

"Well, that's good. For you. I've never tattooed a pussy, but I'm not above trying." Jayden curls his lip. "Where did he touch you?"

I try to unscramble my brain. I don't even remember.

Jayden squeezes harder, and I gasp.

That's right. The man pinned my wrists above my head. My eyesight is starting to narrow.

"My wrists," I try to suck in a breath.

Jayden yanks me forward, and all I can tell is that I'm flying through the air. "Cole, hold her down."

When I blink a few times, clearing my vision, I've landed on my back, and I'm laying on the bed. I scramble to get up, but Cole's heavy hands land on my shoulders, pinning me back down.

Jayden looms at the edge of the bed, his dick hard again despite having already fucked my throat raw. He grips his cock, jerking himself roughly. "You let another man touch what you knew was ours?"

I try to get up, but Cole just leans into me more. "Daddy's talking. Listen up."

Jayden strokes himself harder. "You're ours, Jo. Ours to torment. Ours to fuck with. Ours to own. No one else fucking touches you."

The words cause anger to burn through me. "I'm not yours," I spit.

"No?" Jayden fixes me with a look. "Then prove it. Walk away." His lips curl up in the tiniest smirk.

His mockery burns under my skin. I do a crunch to get my feet up and over my head, but Cole swings his leg over my hips, sitting on me and pinning my hips down.

"Go ahead. Prove you're not ours. Leave." Jayden is slowly stroking himself over my face.

I swipe out at him, but he's already taking a step back.

Cole chuckles, reaching out and flicking Jayden's abs. "There. Got him for you, lemon drop."

"Let me go." I struggle against Cole, trying to wiggle my hips out from under him. His dick is hard against me, and I eye it. I could punch it to get him off me.

Cole sees what I'm looking at, and he has my hands pinned above my head faster than I can register. "Easy, now. No claws in the Crown Jewels."

"Fuck you." I squirm.

Jayden steps closer again. "I don't know, Cole. Seems like she doesn't want to leave, does she?"

I snarl at Jayden, wanting him to get close enough so I can bite his dick off.

Jayden smacks my cheek hard enough to make my eyes water. "There's those pretty tears. Look at you. Helpless as a kitten." He groans, throwing his head back. His whole body stiffens, and he looks down at me. "You're ours. You'll always be ours."

With a groan, Jayden jacks himself off until he's spurting hot cum all over my face. Cole shifts his grip, and before I know it, Jayden is coming on my wrists, too.

Jayden makes sure to get every last drop on me, then steps back. "Better hide, kitten or you might never see the light of day again."

JAYDEN

2

Jo looks so pretty covered in my cum. She's lying under Cole, seething, jaw clenched, nostrils flaring. She's so beautiful and feisty.

So utterly fucking *stupid*.

"Keep her there," I demand, snatching up Jo's phone and marching back over to them. Rage courses through me. Jo thought she could let another man touch her.

My legs tremble. I've had nightmares for the last six months that someone else would touch her. Hurt her. Take advantage of her. She's rash and untrained—an easy target. She was a fucking idiot for letting anyone that close.

Only *we* can be that close. Only *we* can break her.

"Look at me," I demand.

"What?" Jo's gaze snaps from the phone to my eyes. Her eyes are full of challenge and hate, and there's not the slightest bit of submission in them. Immediately, she looks away again.

I lean down, my words slower. "Look. At. Me. I'm going to take a picture, and you will post it so all your little followers know who you belong to."

Jo's eyes flare with anger, and she glares to the side.

"Does someone need a little motivation?" Cole pins Jo's hands in one of his and reaches down between their bodies. Jo jumps when he tweaks her clit.

"Need me to show you just what he wants?" Cole rubs her firmly, steadily, just how we know she likes it.

"No."

"C'mon. Give us those eyes. You know we will make you submit anyway, so you may as well give it willingly."

Jo's hips buck up, either to get away or to chase the sensation. She's already swollen and red after hours of fucking, and she's obviously overstimulated.

Despite the fact I just came, my dick bobs.

"Good girl. What a good fucking girl," Cole says, and Jo lets out a puff of air. Her back is arched, her eyes are closed, and she's covered in pearls of cum. She's beautiful and trapped and *ours*. Fucking hell.

Jo struggles to get out of Cole's hold, always fighting, always running.

My dick bobs painfully, even while anger fills me.

"Jo," Cole tsks. "If you don't come while watching him, I'll make you come all night. It's going to hurt if it doesn't already."

Jo moans a little as if in confirmation.

It has to hurt. A pulse of pleasure runs through me.

"Give him those pretty eyes," Cole croons, continuing to play with her. Her hips buck again, and she glances at him, then down at my waist. Her eyes shift like she's trying to decide if she's going to obey.

I stroke my dick. Again. I hope she doesn't obey. I want to hear her cry and beg under Cole's fingers until she breaks.

And she will break.

Jo fixes her hate-filled eyes on me for a second, and triumph runs through me.

Then, she closes them.

"Jo," Cole warns.

"I looked at him, fucker." Jo squirms.

Cole glances at me.

I want to both laugh and beat her ass. If Jo wants to come all night, she can come all night. I'll enjoy her misery.

"Fuck you." Jo explodes, coming on Cole's fingers while squeezing her eyes shut. Her cheeks are pink, and her lips parted.

"What a naughty girl," Cole moans. I groan, jerking myself off, coming again, but it's not satisfying. I shift so I can mark Jo's wrists again. Where that fucker touched her. The fucker, who should be dead right now. Even more anger fills me.

I snap a few pictures of Jo's face—bright, flushed, and hot with pleasure and hate. Although, she still won't look at me.

"Fuck, Jo. We're going to have so much fun tonight." Cole rocks against her body, grabbing his dick and coming on her stomach. He groans deeply. "Well, I am. You might beg for the first time in your life."

I straighten, grab my boxers, and throw them on. Cole is still braced over her, panting.

Jo still hasn't opened her eyes. "Get fucked, Cole."

He shudders out a laugh, pulling off her. Finally, Jo opens her eyes and reaches to wipe the cum from her.

"Don't touch it," I order, snatching up Jo's phone. "You want your phone so bad? Use it. Post the picture."

Jo narrows her eyes.

I find a picture where she's mid-orgasm, covered in cum, and Cole and I are only visible as shadowed limbs. I send the rest of the images to myself. I turn the phone around. "Post it. With the caption: 'It's so good to be owned.'"

Jo glances between us. I shove it into her hands. Cole scoots next to her so he can see what she's doing.

"To your old account," I say.

People still think Jo's missing. The cops still think she's missing. She's not missing. Not anymore. It's time to get them off our asses.

"I don't...I don't remember the password." Jo goes to wipe her wrist, and I arch an eyebrow.

She stops.

"Find it," I demand.

Jo looks down at her phone. She's silent for a bit, typing, then there's soft, familiar music, and she glances back up at me. "This is the song you chose when you posted for me?"

It's F.Y.B.F. by MC BXB, but Jo plays it anyway—as if I need reminding like I haven't relentlessly stalked her old account in the last six months just to see her face again.

I glare at her. "Yes?"

She glares back at me. "It's stupid."

"For fuck's sake, Jo." I shoot her a look. "Just post the damn picture. Put in your caption that you were taking some well-deserved time off."

I thought the song I chose was great.

Cole swirls his hand in the cum on her stomach, then dips it down to her pussy. "Or, I could post it myself and, as punishment for not obeying, post another for every time I make you come." He pushes his finger inside her. "This poor pussy could use a bit more lube. I'll come inside you again; just give me a minute."

Jo looks down, and panic flares in her eyes. I stiffen. What is she afraid of?

Cole also stiffens, and then realization flashes in his gaze. "We, uhhh, we both got snipped while you were gone."

Oh shit. She's worried about getting pregnant.

Jo looks between us as if trying to determine if Cole is lying. Despite myself, something odd twinges in my heart. We wouldn't lie to her about that.

Jo glares at us, then taps on the phone and seems to accept the answer. Cole rests his head on her shoulder.

"Done." Jo snaps and throws the phone down. "Anything else I can do for your highnesses?"

Oh, she's just begging to be punished. I growl her name when my phone buzzes in my hand.

> Unknown number: Hey, it's Jon from PD. I don't know where you are, but they're doing a raid on Cole's place. Found handcuffs and women's clothes.

> Unknown number: They got search warrants for your phone's GPS. They know you and Cole were at Sage's place the night she disappeared.

> Unknown number: They have cadaver dogs, Jay. Please tell me you're not wrapped up in this.

MY ENTIRE BODY TENSES.

> Unknown number: I'm wiping this phone. Do the same to yours. They can't know I contacted you.

> Unknown number: Consider our debt even. I really hope this has nothing to do with you. Keep your head down, man.

I STARE AT MY PHONE, a sinking feeling spreading through me.

They're coming after us. They're coming after Cole.

After Jo.

My entire body tenses.

I just got her back, and they're trying to take her away. I haven't had time to punish her for leaving us, dig into her pretty little brain, and figure out why the hell she keeps fighting.

And now, I might not.

Which is fucking unacceptable.

COLE

3

WHATEVER JAYDEN'S LOOKING AT ON HIS PHONE HAS HIM frozen.

I immediately straighten. "What is it?"

Jayden doesn't answer, then flashes me a weird look. "Nothing."

The hairs on the back of my neck prickle. Whatever it is, it's bad enough that he can't get his unaffected mask back in place.

I throw on some pants, then jerk my head toward the hallway. "Jo, stay," I order. I grab her phone and take mine with me, too.

Jayden walks stiffly to the door. I grab a keycard and follow him. Just outside the room, Jayden stops. "The window."

"She can't open it." I turn to face him. "What's going on?"

Jayden shakes his head. "It's nothing. I'll take care of it."

Anger fills me, and I get in his face. "We aren't kids anymore, Jay. You don't have to protect me. Tell me what's going on."

Jayden's dark eyes bounce between mine. There's real fear in them, and that shakes me deeply. Jayden is never afraid, and he has never been afraid in all the years we grew up together.

Jayden grips his phone and then hands it to me. "You're on the cop's radar."

"What?" I look over the messages, and my stomach drops.

"Goddamn it." Jayden runs his hands through his hair. "Fuck! I should have told you to leave your phone."

Shit. They're going to find Sage. And Pat.

I try to shrug. "Fine. We just won't go back."

"They'll put warrants out on us. On you." Jayden's face starts to fall back into his mask. The same one he wore when we were kids. The one he wore when I wanted to lose my shit and scream at Pat. When he would calm me down and tell me he'd take care of it. The one where he becomes a different person for weeks. Distant. Unreachable. Angry.

"You'll get arrested," Jayden says.

"Hey, no. It'll be fine." I reach out to grab Jayden's arm, watching him disassociate further into whatever mind prison he retreats to.

"Jay," I snap. "I'm a big boy. I'll be fine."

He gives me a blank look.

I try to get him back. "So what? We'll have warrants and have to stay under the radar. Big deal."

Jayden's eyes flash to me. "With what money, Cole? It's expensive to stay under the radar."

"I don't know! We'll figure something out." I cross my arms. I hate when Jayden wears the weight of the world. He stopped doing it so much when we first got Jo, but he fell back into it as soon as she left.

I search for an answer that'll make him feel better. He's right; we don't have a lot of money. Jayden hasn't worked in a while, and I've worked odd jobs here and there, but we live frugally.

Jayden asks the question that I just started to think about. "What about your mom?"

I wince. My mom cut me off a few months ago, and although

she still lets me stay at the cabin, the extra cash she sent has been gone. I rub the back of my neck. "Yeah...I don't think that's happening."

Jayden watches me. "What do you mean?"

I stare down the empty hall. I didn't tell Jayden that Mom cut me off. He didn't need the extra stress while we were looking for Jo.

"Cole..." There's a warning in his tone.

There's a thump behind our door and the telltale sound of a slide lock being engaged. Both of us freeze.

Did Jo just...lock us out?

I scan the keycard and try to open the door. It catches on the chain hinge.

I glance at Jayden.

That minx just locked us out.

Jo

4

"Mary," Jayden's voice is low in warning.

I cross my arms, glaring at the door. He hasn't called me Mary since the beginning. The door rattles. The chain lock holds it shut.

"What, you don't like it when someone takes away your choice?" My legs tremble, but I stand my ground. I searched through their bags while they were talking and threw their shit around when I didn't find a phone or keys.

I know it was stupid, but the idea of them silencing my voice makes me angry. I fucking chose to come back with them.

This is not how this is going to go.

The door rattles as a huge body presses against it. The lock holds, but I take a step back.

A body slams into the door with a startling bang. Cole's voice comes through the crack, low and soft. "Better hide, Jo. Because when we get our hands on you, nothing will stop us from teaching you a goddamn lesson."

Goosebumps crawl up my arms, moving over the back of my neck. I glance at the old hotel phone. "Maybe I'll just call the cops. Stop this right here and now."

Deadly silence follows.

"Do you have a death wish?" Jayden growls.

My stomach drops out. I turn back to the phone, looking at it again.

Would he actually kill me? Like Sage? Suddenly, I feel like I did when we first met—afraid.

Another slam into the door makes me jump. "If you touch that phone, you'll be begging us for mercy."

Heat rolls through me. I don't fucking beg.

I reach to grab the phone just as the door crashes open. Both men come darting into the room.

Yelping, I jump over the bed to get as far away from them as possible. I spin around. Both slow once they see I'm not close to the phone.

Cole smirks. "I thought I told you to hide, lemon drop."

Every nerve ending lights on fire hearing that old nickname. "And I thought I told you to give me my phone."

Cole laughs, his eyes flaring with challenge. "Oh, you're just begging to be tortured. If you wanted to come all night long, you could have just asked." He takes a slow step toward me.

"No time." Jayden starts throwing their things together. "Grab her, and let's go."

Cole watches me with a predator's stare but doesn't step any closer. "We have some games to play, Jay."

"Not now." Jayden throws a backpack at Cole. "It doesn't take long to check our GPS's. We need to ditch the phones and get a new car."

Their GPS? Get a new car? What is going on?

I glance between the men. Jayden packs the last of the stuff I threw around the room.

Cole's gaze narrows. "Fine. C'mon, little one."

"Wait, where are we going?" I step back.

Neither of them answer me. Cole's gaze softens. "Punishment later, obedience now. We'll keep you safe."

"Safe?" I don't like the way they look fully serious now. "Safe from what? What's going on?" Aren't they the ones I need to be safe from?

Cole walks over to me. I straighten and stare him down. He snatches my hand. "Jay thinks the cops are after us."

My stomach clenches. For what? For kidnapping me? For Sage? I know they know she's missing. I'd stalked her family religiously in the last six months. Listened to them talk about how Sage missed work, and that same day, they'd found her home empty – except for her dog. The news had thrown Jayden's name out there, but everything had died down besides some outraged posts on social media.

Cole's warm hand grabs mine. "C'mon. Wanna learn how to hotwire a car?"

JAYDEN

5

8 *YEARS OLD*

"Suck my dick," Cole says, smashing the keys on the Gameboy.

A cold feeling fills me, and I smack his hand. "Where did you learn to talk like that?"

"Fuck, Jay, don't make me mess up." Cole focuses intently on the screen and leans into the game, missing a stack of blocks on the lineup. His blonde hair flops into his eyes. It's always long and untrimmed, bleached from the summer sun. The screen flashes, and Cole's score fills the background.

"Son of a crack whore." Cole throws his arms back dramatically. "You're beating me every time."

I swallow roughly.

I know Cole is losing on purpose. He asked me why I'd been so quiet recently and if I wanted to play. He also asked about my black eye. I told him it came from a kid at school. He's in the grade below me, so he doesn't know any better.

"You gonna play?" Cole asks, looking at me hopefully.

I manage a smile. I'll try to play along. I can't stand to see him upset.

I play the next round and get more points than him. Cole throws himself against the couch dramatically again. Despite myself, I crack a tiny smirk, which only encourages Cole more. He gets more and more dramatic, drawing more of a reaction from me.

I never laugh. Not recently, anyway.

A rich voice rips through the house. "Why in the hell is it so loud in here?"

I jump, my stomach immediately in my throat. Pat stands in the doorway, and instantly, I stop playing.

Pat stalks in. He looks happy, which is never a good thing.

"Who the fuck left the back door open?"

Silence. I see Cole's face fall from the corner of my eye.

Before he can say anything, I say, "I did."

Cole sucks in a breath, and I reach my hand down to pinch his thigh. I've done everything I can to keep Pat away from him recently. I've seen him watching Cole with the same eyes he gives me.

I feel sick.

"Really," Pat says dryly.

"I'm sorry," I say.

"Sorry isn't going to cut it. You think I'm trying to keep the whole neighborhood cool? AC isn't cheap." Pat steps closer. "Get the hell upstairs."

I move to obey, but Cole puts his hand out. "Jay—"

"Fuck off," I hiss. Maybe all Pat will do is whoop me. If that's it, I don't care. I can handle a whooping.

I move to the steps, and Pat hesitates, looking back at Cole. For a moment, pure terror runs through me. He's going to target Cole.

I need to do something. Anything.

I try to speak, but my body is locked in fear. I'm frozen.

I can't move. Why can't I move?

Pat stares at Cole, watching him. His light blue eyes look him up and down, and I want to throw up.

Finally, Pat turns to me. "Get the fuck upstairs, boy."

I jump to obey. I practically fly up the stairs, and Pat follows me to his room.

"You know, I try to raise you better than this." He shuts the door behind us and slowly pulls his belt from the loops. "Try to be the father you never had."

I might throw up. I've never seen Pat look at Cole like that. I should have distracted him. Shouted something. Hit him. Run. *Anything.*

But all I did was stand there.

"Turn around."

I obey. I pull my shirt off, staring at the wall. I will him to get this over with and lean my stomach against the bed like he always asks. Like a zombie, I obey without a fight. Like always.

Pat lays the belt into me, whooping my back and ass with all his strength. Sometimes, he gets his belt wet to make it hurt more, but not today. The more of a reaction I give him, the harder he hits, so I stay silent.

When he's done, Pat runs his hands over the welts.

"Now, now, what am I going to do with you, Jayden? I don't think you were being honest with me."

I can't keep the shiver off my hot skin. Fuck.

Pat chuckles. It's throaty and deep, and I always thought he sounded like Santa. Now, I can't stand the holiday.

"I think Cole left that door open. Think he shouldn't have that stupid fucking game that distracts you guys so much. Then maybe I wouldn't lose so much goddamn money raising ungrateful brats."

My heart sinks. Cole loves that game.

I open my mouth to say something, but nothing comes out.

Pat chuckles like he does when he senses weakness.

Fuck. I've fucked up. I clear my throat.

"Hmmm." Pat continues rubbing. My skin is on fire from the belt, and his light touch feels good—and I hate that.

"Are you willing to take the consequences for that door?"

I grit my teeth. I just got the consequences. Pat's hands run lower, tracing over my ass and thighs.

It's like my voice is trapped. All I want to do is scream yes. To say I'll take it. To fight him. To get out of here.

Pat laughs; his chuckle is hearty and deep. "Good boy. Good fucking boy. Despite everything, I love you, Jayden. I really do."

The rip of his zipper follows, and I completely disassociate, doing nothing. I can't do anything. I'm stuck. Frozen.

Fucking silent.

JAYDEN

6

I follow Cole and Jo out to the hotel parking lot. Cole is damn near cheerful, telling Jo all the different steps to stealing and hotwiring a car. He demonstrates on the car he picked—a mid-size, black SUV that looks like every other car on the road.

I know Cole is putting on a show for me, trying to cheer me up, but I can't be cheerful. When his name popped up on those texts, I felt the familiar numbness creep back in.

I've spent my whole life trying to make sure Cole stays out of my trouble. This time, I've been too careless, and now it's going to ruin Cole's and Jo's lives.

Again.

Emotions overwhelm me, and I swallow roughly. Fucking hell. I haven't felt things in so long. Now, for the past few months, I've been feeling everything I thought I locked away for so long. I can't sleep. Can't think. All of the feelings are rattling inside my brain so loudly that it's all I can do to keep them silent.

Jo did that to me. She made me feel again, and I fucking hate it. My throat hurts, and I look desperately for a distraction.

When she thinks Cole isn't looking, Jo looks over her shoulder at the main road. She sees me watching, and her eyes dart quickly away.

She's thinking about running.

I feel familiar anger wash over me. We just got her back, and she's trying to run? After all she put us through to find her? Again?

The anger calms and grounds me. I know anger. It's been the only thing to keep me safe all these years.

When Jo glances around again and locks eyes with me, I smirk.

Her gaze sours, and it makes a pulse of pleasure run down to my dick. I forgot how expressive she is. How easy it is to see every emotion on her face.

She ought to know better than to let the predators sense weakness.

But she's reckless and wants to keep fighting me.

My skin feels hot. I want to dissect her brain. Figure out why she won't stop fighting us when anyone else would have given up and shown me their belly. I want to break her slowly to find out. Lay out all her little pieces and sort them into piles. Will she cry? Scream? Withdraw?

Wishful thinking. She'll never withdraw. The only time she ever came close was when I first brought her back to the cabin. And she wasn't doing anything. She was studying me. Analyzing my weaknesses. Fighting.

I want to know why Jo won't stop fucking fighting. And I'll find out.

There's no more running from me. No more hiding.

She can't escape me, and I'm here to make her life a living fucking hell.

COLE

7

I grab Jo's petite hand and pull her into the backseat with me. Jayden drives. I know he needs some feeling of control. He always gets like this when he's stressed—controlling and quiet. I hoped I'd never see that again once we got Jo back.

"Where are we going?" Jo tries to pull away from me, and I yank her back, putting her hand over my crotch. As she struggles to get away, it makes my dick harden immediately.

Jo's angry eyes fly to mine in the darkness. I pull her forward and kiss those little pursed lips.

Jo makes a cry of surprise, and I lean into her further, licking her soft mouth and nearly groaning at her taste. She tastes sweet and addictive, and I just can't get enough. I prod past her lips and swoop my tongue in.

Jo leans in and tries to bite me.

I pull back, chuckling. "If you bite me, I'll fuck you right here for anyone to see."

Jo lets loose another delicious gasp. Fucking hell, I'm hard as stone. I didn't think it was possible, after all the fucking we did, but this woman does something to me.

Jo's hand squeezes on my dick, and she digs her fingers in. A sharp bite of pain shoots up my body, and I moan, bucking my hips into her.

"Oh, you like that?" Jo grips again, harder.

I groan. Yes. Yes, I fucking like that.

Jo leans into my ear. "Well, if you want me to touch you again, you'll tell me where we're going."

Her hand squeezes just right, but not enough.

Fucking hell, I love this bossy side of her. "I don't know, little one."

Jo makes a sound of disgust and pulls away.

"Wait." I snap my hand out to grab her chin, making her face me. "I really don't know. We can't go back to the cabin. Cops are crawling all over it."

I meet Jo's gaze until she stops fighting me. Her eyes soften a bit. "Oh."

I know what we have to do. I have to grovel to my mom. And I'd rather do anything but that. I already know she won't pick up the phone if I call her.

I kiss Jo again, just to see her reaction. She frowns, and it makes me smile. Fuck, I missed her.

Jayden pulls into a rest stop.

"We already out of gas?" I look over his shoulder at the fuel gauge.

"Need to swap the plates out," Jayden says. "Look for a car that's the same make and model."

I scan the lot as he drives, but I want to look at Jo. Soak her in until she's imprinted in my vision, and all I see is her.

Jayden growls, "Gonna call your mom?"

I lean back, spreading my legs out and clasping my hands behind my head. "Gonna stop acting like an asshole?"

Jayden glares at me.

I shrug. "I'll take that as a no."

He narrows his eyes. "Make the call."

He sees right through my act. He always does.

"Cole," Jayden says.

I clench my jaw. "I can't, Jayden. Because she married Ralph. Is that what you want to hear?"

Jayden immediately tenses. We're driving past the rows of cars on another lap, and the whole car is silent.

Jayden lets out a long breath. Ralph was Pat's friend. Longtime friend and full-time weirdo. He's a pastor for a mega church in our old area. Even thinking about him reminds me of Pat. It throws me into memories I try so hard to forget. Which is part of the reason I refuse to talk to my mother.

Fuck. My hands start to sweat.

Jo's stomach growls. I snap my gaze at her. Even in the low light from the rising sun, I see her pale cheeks.

Of course she's hungry. We forgot to fucking feed her.

A horrible feeling cramps through my stomach. How could we forget that?

I motion to the fast food place attached to the gas station. "Jay, swing in there, and let's get some food."

Jayden glances back at us. I see the inner debate in his mind: a stolen car, warrants, a missing woman, witnesses.

"I'm fine," Jo grumbles.

"No, you're not." I glare at Jayden. "Go, Jay."

He glances between us again.

"Fuck man, we have to eat sometime." There's venom in my voice. We don't have much food in the car. We hadn't planned on running. This whole thing is so fucked up.

Jayden relents, and we pull in line.

"What do you want?" I ask Jo.

"Ten-piece chicken nuggets with a Sprite," Jayden rattles off.

The car gets silent. That's the last order she gave us in the hospital before she ran. Jayden rehearsed every detail after she got away. As if that would somehow bring her back.

Jo glances at us, suddenly looking shy. "Uh, yeah."

I nod. "What else? That's not enough."

She pauses. "Uh, I guess a burger?"

I say, "Make it two. And fries. And a milkshake."

Jayden nods. As he pulls up to grab our order, I pull Jo to me and smother her in a kiss. Both to hide her face and keep her from doing something stupid. She fights me, but I don't let her up until we're past that window. When we get our food, we drive to a part of the lot where we're out of sight of the cameras and Jayden parks.

Jo is still sputtering, but she tries to grab a bag of food.

"No," I lightly smack it away. "I'm going to feed you."

Jo pulls back with a horrified look on her face. "What?"

I chuckle. "I'm. Going. To. Feed. You." I open the box of nuggets. "Now be a good girl and open up."

Jo leans back further, a flush on her cheeks. "That's stupid, I can feed myself."

"I know you can, you stubborn woman." I arch an eyebrow. "Let me do this."

Jo clamps her lips shut.

"This isn't a choice." I raise an eyebrow. Am I going to have to force her to let me take care of her?

My dick twitches at the idea. Yeah, I think I'd like that.

"Is anything a choice with you guys?" Jo's pretty blue eyes look between me and the food.

"No." I grin.

Jo's face twists in a pretty little snarl. However, her stomach growls again. Loudly.

She huffs and crosses her arms. "Fine."

I grin wider. "Open that pretty little mouth."

Jo hesitates, then does – partially. Like she's embarrassed or unsure of how far to open it.

I wink at her and slide the nugget in. "Bite."

She does, pulling back immediately and glancing down.

Her submission goes straight to my dick, and I harden fully. Fucking hell, this woman affects me by barely doing anything.

I'm fucking ruined for her.

Jo takes the next bite more willingly, taking the rest of the nugget. I see the hunger in her face now.

I chuckle. "See? No reason to fight me at every turn, Jo."

Jo's gaze immediately hardens. "I'm only doing it because you wouldn't let me eat otherwise."

"Shhhh." I put another bite in her mouth. "That's a good girl. You're catching on quickly."

When she's swallowed, she goes to say something else, but I push some more fries in her mouth instead. Jo lets loose a little moan, and her eyes roll back in her head. My dick pulses.

"Jesus," comes softly from the front seat. Jayden's eyes are fixed in the mirror, watching us.

I grab the drink and give it to Jo. She wraps her lips around the straw eagerly and sucks it down. Fuck, what I wouldn't do to have her lips around me that enthusiastically.

When Jo's done with her drink, she glances at the bags of food. "More."

I chuckle and continue feeding her. I put my fingers close enough to the edge of the food, so her lips brush them every time she takes a bite.

Precum leaks into my pants, and every shift sends a thrill through me. The woman who fights us at every turn is letting me take care of her. I know it's because she's starving, but for a second, I let myself imagine it's because she trusts me.

I want her to trust me.

Jo leans back, rubbing her stomach. "Fuck, I'm stuffed."

"Not done." I reach for the milkshake. We fucked her all night, and she has our initials carved into her arm. She needs more. The pill I gave her should be helping with the pain, but she needs energy to heal.

"Too much," Jo tries to wave me off.

"No," I level my glare at her. "At least a few bites."

Jo groans but opens for my spoonful. I watch her lips close over the spoon, pulling every last bit away. I watch her delicate neck bob as she swallows.

Jayden shifts in the front seat, adjusting himself.

I smirk at him. "Eyes on the cars, loverboy. We're looking for a plate, remember?"

Jayden shoots me a dark glare, then turns back to face the front, muttering, "I found her first; just remember that."

I arch an eyebrow. "Oh wow, how very second grade of you." I turn to Jo, a devious thought filling my mind. "Who would you pick if you had to pick one of us?"

Jo tries to grab the milkshake in my hand. "Neither. Give me that."

I laugh, pulling it back out of her reach. "Pick!"

"Fucking hell!" Jo slumps back into her seat. "You're both insufferable assholes who kidnapped me...twice."

I shrug. "Okay, grumpy. We can revisit this argument after you've had some sleep." I wink at her. "But I know it's me."

Jo shakes her head, and I put the milkshake within her reach. I don't really care who she'd pick. She doesn't have a choice to pick anyone but the two of us. But still, I like getting a rise out of both of them.

Leaning back into the trunk, I rustle through my bag. When I find what I'm looking for, I turn back around. "Close your eyes and open your mouth."

Jo snorts. "Fuck no."

I chuckle. "While I'd highly recommend you *not* do that if Jayden asks you to, you're safe with me."

Jayden shoots me a dangerous look.

Jo's gaze bounces between my eyes. "What is it?"

"It's a treat. You'll like it."

For the longest time, I don't think she'll trust me, and my heart squeezes. She doesn't trust me.

I try to reason with myself. Try to talk back the murderous anger that fills me. Just as I'm about to force her jaw open, Jo relents, looking exhausted. She closes her eyes and opens her mouth.

Fucking hell. If that isn't the prettiest sight. I drop the treat in. Instantly, Jo opens her eyes again, sucking on it. "What...it's...a lemon drop?"

I wink at her. The tiniest crack of a smile reaches Jo's eyes before she covers it again. She's well-fed and tired. I'm feeling it myself, too.

"Come here." I reach for Jo, pulling her into me so she can rest on me and sleep.

As I expected, she tries to pull away.

"Shhh," I stroke her arm, keeping her pinned to my side. "Rest."

Jo continues trying to fight for a bit, but I don't let her get anywhere. Finally, she huffs and relaxes against me.

She won't submit to me willingly. Right now. But I'm a patient man.

I'll break her down.

She should probably keep trying to hide from me. Because once I have her heart, I'll never give it back.

Even if she begs.

COLE

8

Jo passes out, and Jayden finds a suitable plate. He makes the swap smoothly, and we leave right after. The driver with the stolen plates probably won't even know the difference. If the cops run our plates now, the car won't come back stolen, and it'll match our car type close enough not to raise red flags.

After we hit the road again, Jayden says, "You need sleep."

The peaceful hum of the tires fills the car, and I continue stroking Jo's hair. "So do you."

Jayden grunts. "I'll be fine."

I glare at him. He always tries to pull this shit. The tough, big brother I-don't-need-anything shit. "No, you won't. Pull over somewhere, and we'll sleep."

Jayden's eyes are heavy with sleep and worry. I'm also feeling the adrenaline crash after finding Jo and having to run from the cops. Fuck. I knew this would happen eventually, but I didn't want it to happen now.

Jayden looks in the mirror. "You nap, then we'll switch out."

"Fine," I mutter. Jo's warm body on mine and the rumble of the engine lulled me quicker than I thought. At some point, I pass out.

. . .

"COLE. How's my favorite boy doing?"

I wince. Pat comes into the living room. I'm sick today after spending the night with Jayden, so I stayed at his place instead of going to school.

Pat ruffles my hair. "Getting into all kinds of trouble, I'm sure?"

I glare at him. My throat feels awful, and I'm not in the mood.

Not that I ever am.

"Just you and me today, buddy." Pat steps close enough to me that his crotch is in my face.

I scoot away. "I don't feel good."

Pat's demeanor changes. "You haven't played the game in weeks."

I glare at the couch cushion, staring at it with as much hate as I feel for this man.

"Cole," he says warningly.

I feel hot. Every time I've fought him, it's gotten worse for me.

"Cole." Pat slides next to me. "This game needs to be played regularly. There are bad side effects when that tension isn't released."

I still ignore him.

"I'll be forced to find others to play the game with."

I freeze.

"Jayden would be a good boy for me, don't you think?"

Fear rushes through me. No! No, no, no. I don't want Jayden to go through this, either.

I snap my gaze to Pat.

He grins. "Ah, there's my boy again. Feeling better?"

I glare at him. I hate this man more than anything.

One day, when I'm bigger, I'm going to kill him. I will make him feel all the things that he made me feel. And I'm going to drag it out.

"Good boy," Pat flips out a knife. "Now show me your back. I'll bet it's all healed from last time."

I STARTLE AWAKE. My breathing is heavy, and my heart races as I look around. I'm in the car. Jo's asleep with her head on my lap. Instantly, I relax a little. I'm safe. It was just a dream.

I stroke Jo's hair for a while until the car's hum and the exhaustion pull me back under.

9

TWELVE YEARS OLD

My ears ring, and dust fills my mouth. I cough as the world around me comes into focus. I'm lying on the ground, the ATV is upside down, and my whole chest hurts.

I flipped the ATV.

A small hit of exhilaration runs through me. Fuck, that was fun. Dad's going to kill me. My adrenaline mounts.

I stand up, moving over to the machine. It's still running while upside down. I glance over my shoulder at the house. Mom can see me from the front window. I wish she'd pay attention to me. Just this once. Maybe she'd be all worried about me. Ask if I was hurt. Bustle around me like a mother hen, put a bandaid on my scrapes, and kiss my forehead.

Yeah, I'm being stupid.

I try to flip the ATV back over, but eventually, I flop down, my arms and legs shaking and sweat rolling down me. I skinned up my hands and right shoulder, but otherwise, I'm fine. The sun is getting lower in the sky when I hear my dad driving down the road.

I wait for him. Flipping the ATV made me feel alive for a second, but it's already starting to fade. I need more.

The car stops, and a door slams. "Mary!"

I get to my feet.

"Mary!" Dad runs up, grabbing me by the shoulders and picking me up. "Are you okay? What happened?"

"I'm fine."

Dad checks me all over. "What the hell happened? Are you sure you're okay?"

"I'm okay!" I yank away from him.

Dad steps back, looking over the ATV. He runs his hands through his hair. "Mary. I told you not to drive this while I was gone!"

He did tell me that. But I wanted to feel the wind in my hair. To do something that made me feel alive. Plus, he rarely pays attention to what I do anyway. No one does. Until I fuck up.

Dad looks the ATV over. "Fuck. You fucked it up."

A slight grin tugs at my mouth, and that confuses me. This is bad. Wrong. I flipped the ATV, and he's mad.

But he's here. He's saying more than a distracted: how's school? And how're those grades? A mix of emotions fills me, but none of them are loneliness.

Dad glances over at me. Before I can duck, his hand hits my face so hard it jerks me to the side. Pain explodes up my cheek, and I want to throw up.

I suck in a breath. Dad has never hit me before.

"Don't smirk at me. And never disobey me."

I blink the tears out of my eyes as rage fills me. I grin, shaking my arms out. Electricity runs through them. Alive. I feel fucking alive.

I whirl on my dad, striking out before he can hit me again,

hitting any part of him I can reach. Exhilaration runs through me. He's going to fucking kill me.

Strong hands grab me, holding my arms still. Dad shakes me, snapping my head back and forth, then brings me up to his face.

"Why do you always fucking disobey?"

"Fuck you," I spit.

Dad shakes me again so hard I get dizzy. My world spins.

Dad sets me down on my feet so hard my stomach jars.

"Brat. You're such a fucking brat." He steps away from me and runs a hand through his hair.

I taste blood, but I've never felt more alive. Dad sees me. I'm a brat, but he sees me.

I heave for breath, and Dad puts his hands on his knees, also gasping.

I straighten. I'm a good driver. I spent years practicing, learning tricks with no one to show them to. I hate to admit it, but I wanted Dad to get off his damn phone and pay attention to me. But he never does. Unless I'm in trouble.

Dad shakes his head and walks away from me. "I love you, Mary. Don't make me do this again."

I want to chase after him. To scream at him to love me. To look at the bruise on my face and care for me.

But he just walks away.

After that, nothing changed. He spent more and more time away. I cried about that for months. I picked more fights with him whenever I could. He hit me every time. And every time, I felt a little more alive while little pieces of me died.

10

I sᴛᴀʀᴛʟᴇ as I'm jostled awake. I blink, trying to figure out where I am.

I take it in slowly. The car. Fuck. Jayden and Cole took me back.

A rush of adrenaline fills me. I sit up slightly, seeing Jayden driving still.

It looks like the middle of the day, and we're out in the middle of nowhere. Jayden doesn't see me, and his eyes are heavy. His head droops, and the tires rumble over the strips on the side of the road.

"Shit," Jayden cusses, and I jump.

I'm still exhausted, and now my arm hurts like a bitch. My head hurts, too. The more I wake up, the more reality sets in, and my heart starts to pound.

I'm back with the men. They're mean and unforgiving and exactly like they were in the cabin. With a little bit of sleep, I see the red flags. I'd rehearsed meeting them again in the mirror, and in my mind, there were nothing but green flags. In my mind, I stood up for myself, and they opened up to me. Even groveled a little. Treated me like an equal.

Which is certainly not what they're doing now.

I swallow. What the hell am I doing? I feel more alive than ever, but I'm shacking up with someone who kills their exes.

Am I an ex to Jayden after I ran? Does that mean he'll kill me too?

I don't even know where we're going.

My heart starts racing again. Cole moans and tightens his warm grip on me. I lay back down, pretending to be asleep.

"Fuck it," Jayden mutters from the front seat. I feel the car veer off the side of the road, and immediately, we bump along like we're on dirt.

Cole's breathing changes, and then his voice rumbles over me, "Where are we?"

I keep my eyes shut.

"Cattle field. I'm gonna nap. Go back to sleep."

Cole moans. "I can drive."

"No, you're exhausted. It's better to drive at night anyway."

Cole grumbles, and I feel his hand tracing up and down my arm.

We slow to a stop, and Jayden lets out a big sigh.

The car is quiet, then Cole mumbles, "Where are you going?"

"Your mom's house."

Cole huffs. "Good one."

"Seriously. I tried calling her, but she didn't pick up."

Cole huffs again. He's silent for a minute, then asks, "You okay?"

"Of course I fucking am."

"Okay, well, you just seem...like, I don't know. Before."

"Jesus, Cole. Just get some sleep."

"Just don't let it be a problem. You'll scare Jo off."

Jayden just grunts.

"I'm being serious, dude. We just got her back, and you're kind of being a giant asshole."

"Go to sleep," Jayden growls.

"You know what? Don't say I didn't try," Cole grumbles, running his fingers through my hair and causing a shiver of delight to run through me. "Just don't go back to the old you. I thought we moved past that."

The silence is loud.

Finally, Jayden mutters, "She disobeyed. This is what you get when you disobey."

Adrenaline fills me, and I flash back to my dream. That's exactly what my dad used to say. After he'd kick my ass.

Fuck. None of this is going to get better. I'm just repeating history. Only this time, with a killer.

After some time, Cole's breath evens out under me. As his evens out, mine gets more ragged. Jayden thinks he can just abuse me into compliance. And that's not going to fucking work for me.

Cole isn't safe, either. He'll fuck with me just as fast as Jayden will. He stood by as Jayden killed Sage.

I refuse to believe he'd allow that with me. But still...

I refuse to be the next Sage.

Jayden can kiss my ass. As soon as Jayden falls asleep, I'm out of here. My legs jerk with the need to get away.

The silence in the car feels like it's gone on forever. Jayden leaves the car running, which I don't expect. But it's hot as balls out, and we'd probably cook if he didn't. Finally, I dare a peek up at Jayden. His seat is leaned back, and his breathing is even, slow, and deep. Cole's snoring slightly.

I sit up slowly.

Neither man moves.

I glance around. There's nothing as far as I can see. We are truly out in the middle of nowhere with the sun blazing down on our car. I can see the heat rolling off the ground.

Fuck. I won't last long out there without water. I glance in the trunk. The boys have some bags. Mine is back there, just out of reach, but I know there's water in it.

Do I risk grabbing it, or do I just run?

My heart hammers. If I can just get to a main road, I can flag someone down and get away. Forget the water; I'll do that.

I look at the boys again. Still asleep.

Slowly, painfully slow, I inch away from Cole and reach for the door handle. As slow as I can, I pull the handle toward me.

Nothing.

I try again.

Fuck. Is the...child lock on?

I cuss internally. Fuck, fuck, fuck. This is not good. I'm going to have to crawl over the center console. I'm going to get caught.

I recheck Jayden's breathing. It's slow and steady, his mouth hanging slightly open. Even in sleep, he looks hot as fuck, and that makes me hate him more.

My hands shake, and I bunch them into fists. I should punch him right in that pretty face. But I don't. Only because that means I wouldn't be able to run.

Slowly, I get both my feet under me. If I stand up and step over the console, I can slip out the passenger side.

Slowly, I step my leg over, trying to keep my back from brushing on the roof of the car. I have to turn my back to Jayden, which causes exhilaration to shoot down my spine.

I'm alive. I'm alive and angry again.

It's the high I'll never stop chasing.

The seat's fabric rubs under my shoe as I stand on it. I freeze halfway over.

Nothing.

I step the rest of the way, crouching on the front seat, waiting for one of them to wake up.

Nothing.

I grab the handle and slowly pop it open. It works, and the door cracks open.

Then the car starts dinging.

I jump out of my skin. The car continues to ding with the keys still in the ignition.

Someone shifts behind me, and I launch myself out of the car.

The blistering heat hits me in a wave. I take off in a blind sprint, running as fast as I can. The hot wind rushes past my ears, and I feel like I'm flying.

"Jo!" A deep voice shouts after me.

Fuck! They woke up. I push harder, running in a straight line with nothing in front of me but a pasture full of dry grass. I know that a gravel road or line of asphalt can pop out of nowhere. And maybe a car will come by. Fuck, I need a car to come by.

There's a whoop behind me. "We have a runner, Jay!"

Fucking hell, Jo. I push my legs to go faster.

I hear the rev of an engine. For a second, hope runs through me. Is there a car coming?

I glance over my shoulder. There's a car, but it's our car. Jesus, Jo, how could you be this stupid? You can't outrun a car.

I catch a glimpse of movement off to my right. Cole sprints toward me.

I veer left. The car rushes up beside me.

Cole is herding me in.

Exhilaration runs through me.

I switch directions, darting back the way the car came. Jayden slams on the brakes.

"Nowhere to hide, is there?" Cole changes direction with me.

"Fuck off!"

"Come here, pretty girl." Cole is close enough to take a swipe at me.

I dart away, changing directions again.

"Scream for me again, Jo." Cole heads me off again. When I whirl, I see Jayden is out of the car now.

I dart away from both of them, but Cole sticks to me like a shadow, reaching out occasionally to grab me, constantly pushing me closer to Jayden.

"Give up." Cole has a lazy grin on his face. "You can't run from us."

My heart is racing, and the heat is overwhelming. I gasp for breath. I heave, slowing drastically. Cole slows with me, not even breathing heavily. He walks toward me, and I back up.

A hand grips my arm from behind, and I scream, adrenaline racing through me.

"Got you," Jayden says. "There's that pretty scream of yours."

Jayden shoves me toward Cole, and he catches me, both hands gripping my arms. "Fuck, you sound gorgeous when you're afraid."

"Let me go." I push back against Cole's firm chest.

Cole gives me a mean smile. "Never, Mary Jo Hall. You're mine forever." His blue eyes are alive with fire, and he yanks me close to his face. "The more you run from me, the more I want you." He squeezes me hard enough that pain shoots through my arms.

Jayden's voice barks from behind us, "Put her on her knees."

Cole yanks me around and shoves me down roughly. My knees crack against the ground, and pain shoots up through me as Cole's heavy hands land on my shoulders.

Jayden has something in his hand. It's a...prong collar.

"Clearly, you can't be trusted on your own."

I try to scramble back, but Cole pushes down on me. "No, no. Accept your punishment like a good little pet."

Jayden crouches down so he's at eye level with me. There's nothing in his blank expression. No anger, no hatred, nothing.

It makes chills run through me despite the burning heat.

"Clearly, you need some more training." Jayden lifts the collar to my eye level. He pauses while watching me.

I glare at him.

Jayden's dark eyes flash in a tiny hint of triumph. "This is going to be yours from now on. Don't take it off, don't loosen it, don't touch it."

I sneer at him. "You can't make me do shit."

A slow smile creeps over Jayden's face. He doesn't say anything; he just unhooks one of the links.

As he leans in to put the collar around my neck, I spit on him.

Jayden freezes. The cool metal slides against my skin, and I watch the glob of spit creep down his neck.

Cole breaks the silence by laughing. "Me next, spitfire. Goddamn."

Jayden catches my gaze. There's fire and emotion in it this time. "You're gonna pay for that, kitten."

He fastens the links together, and Cole pulls my hair out from under it. It's snug but not tight, and it doesn't pinch, either.

Jayden clips a leash to the collar, wraps the leash around his fist, and yanks me toward him. Instantly, the collar tightens all the way around my neck like a vise. Jayden holds the pressure, looking down at me with a blank expression.

After a few seconds, I get lightheaded. I blink to keep the spinning down.

Jayden smiles again and releases some of the tension. "Good girl." He stands. "Now, since we can't trust you on your feet —crawl."

What? Hell no. The ground burns me through my leggings.

"It's hot," I hiss.

"Good. It'll teach you not to run."

Cole pats my head. "It makes me hard when you run and even harder when I punish you for it."

"Don't encourage her." Jayden snaps. "Let's go, Jo." He starts walking, pulling the leash with him.

The collar tightens around my neck again, yanking me towards Jayden. I growl as my hands hit the hot dirt. Jayden doesn't let up, forcing me to crawl behind him.

The humiliation roars through me. Rocks dig into my hands and knees, and the summer sun has soaked into the ground, burning me every time I put my hands down. The pressure on the cuts on my arm hurts, too.

Cole walks beside me. I hiss as my knee slips on a rock, and hot pain explodes through me.

"Good girl. Look at you being our obedient slut," Cole says.

I refuse to beg them to stop, so I clench my jaw and keep going. The heat blisters against my skin and the crawl seems to take forever, but finally, the shade of the car falls over me.

I sit back on my knees, panting. I'm hot from the sun, the humiliation, everything. My knee throbs. My arm throbs. My hands throb.

"See, that wasn't so hard." Jayden pops the trunk and reaches inside. "You thirsty?"

I nod. I am. My mouth is dry, and I'm covered in sweat.

Jayden yanks his shirt off, exposing his ripped abs and tattooed chest. He grabs a water bottle and cracks it open. If I had any spit in my mouth, it would have watered.

Jayden comes up beside me. "You ready for your punishment?"

Didn't I just have it? I lick my lips.

Jayden watches my face and chuckles. "That was just some messing around for running. You haven't been punished yet for locking the door on us."

Dread sinks in my stomach.

"Up you go." Jayden grabs me and sits me in the trunk of the car. "Lay down."

I don't like the looks in either of their eyes. They look dark, excited, and mean. At the same time, I can't help but like it.

I scramble to get away, but Cole slides in with me, pulling my pants down and sitting on my hips.

My primitive brain kicks in, and I scramble. I claw and scratch and fight to get away.

"Easy, lemon drop." Cole pins my shoulders down, his face over mine. "Easy, shhhh."

But I won't relax. I won't let them win. "Fuck off! Fucking let me go!"

Jayden grabs my flailing arms.

"Careful of her arm," Cole says.

"I am."

Cole gets my arms from Jayden and pins them to my stomach.

"Eyes on me," Jayden demands. "Cole's gonna fuck you. And you are going to drown for me."

What? I feel the tip of Cole's dick on my pussy.

"No. Fuck you!" A spark of real fear fills me. I fight, but it does no good. Cole pushes in slowly, seating himself inside. I kick and try to thrash away, but he keeps on with his relentless pressure. "That a girl. Let me in."

"Fuck you," I cry. My head is spinning with adrenaline. Despite the slight soreness, I'm horrified to feel how wet I am as he pushes all the way in.

"Now." Jayden grabs a water bottle. "Let's play—you and me."

My gaze snaps to Jayden's. That dark look is still there.

"You want to stop fighting me?"

"Never," I grit my teeth.

Jayden glares at me and throws his shirt over my face. Immediately, I start wrestling to get away.

I thrash. "Let me –"

Water washes over my face, filling my mouth. I cough, trying to suck a breath in, but the wet cloth gets in the way.

I throw my head to the side.

Water. My lungs are full of water.

Pure panic fills me. It hurts to try to breathe. I can't fucking breathe.

There are fuzzy sounds of voices.

I cough, finally getting the water out of my mouth, my chest heaving.

Air. I need fucking air.

I heave for breath, feeling Cole pump in and out of me again. Pressure lands on my clit in slow circles.

"Fuck," I cough.

"Shhh," Jayden croons, "just a little more."

More water floods my face, my mouth, my nose, and again, I can't breathe. My lungs seize up, unable to open. They're flooded.

I thrash my head from side to side, fuzziness filling my mind. I cough the water out again, gasping in a shaky breath.

The fear runs straight to my clit, where soft circles are being rubbed. All the energy pools in that one spot, shooting sensation through me.

"Cole," I gasp.

Jayden moans, "I know, I know...just one more."

Water splashes across my face once more, and again, I can't breathe. I buck and thrash, and all sounds mute. I'm going to drown. I'm going to fucking drown.

Vaguely, I feel the shirt leave my face, and I cough, hacking water out of my lungs. Pressure continues to assault my clit, and my whole body buzzes.

"This is what happens to people who fight me, Jo. I break them."

I suck in my first real breath, and I feel pressure on my ass. I struggle to get away. Fuck I want to breathe!

Strong arms band around my back. "Shhhh. I got you. I'll take care of you."

"We're the only ones who will give you what you need."

Fingers stroke my clit, and pleasure fills me in a wash of sensation. My skin erupts in goosebumps, and I groan.

"That's it, relax into me."

I'm flipped so I'm lying face down on Cole's chest. Something presses into my ass. The wash of sensations hits me all at once. I blink, focusing on the floor of the trunk.

I feel more pressure on my ass. I groan, shifting.

"You're okay," Jayden's voice croons. "Just prepping this pretty little ass to take me."

I blink again. Cole watches me, and when I make eye contact with him, he starts thrusting under me, bringing a hand down to play with my clit.

"I'll make it feel good, Jo."

Despite everything, I clench down, causing pleasure to zip through me.

Cole moans.

Jayden's fingers pull out, and there's pressure against my ass once again.

"Give her a yank, Cole."

Suddenly, there's a tightening around my neck, distracting me from the slight twinge in my ass. "Eyes, little one."

I snap my gaze to Cole's blue eyes. He immediately releases the tension on the collar, causing a whoosh to go through me. "Good girl. Keep those pretty eyes on me."

There's a biting pain in my ass, and I gasp.

"Hey." Cole sharply yanks once. "Focus on me."

I suck in a breath. Jayden groans behind me, and burning pain fills me. "Fuck, kitten. You feel so good. Keep fighting me. It feels good around my dick."

The collar tightens around my neck again, and my head gets

light. My mind starts to empty of anything but pain and pleasure. The sensations war back and forth, getting stronger as Jayden pushes into my ass. I clench down again, my orgasm just around the corner. Spots dance in my vision, and buzzing fills my ears.

Suddenly, Cole lets off the pressure, and rushing blood roars back into my head. I let out a single gasp and come, clenching down on both of them. Wave after wave of euphoria fills me, crashing over me and pulling me down with it. I feel light, buzzing with pleasure and sensation, my head a swimming mix of lights and sounds.

I come for longer than I ever have in my life. I feel Cole tense beneath me, and then Jayden grunts behind me. I feel their hands stroking up and down my body. Their soft voices. Suddenly, I'm sitting up in Cole's lap.

"You did so good, Jo. So fucking good. Did I not say we'd take care of you?"

Suddenly, I'm tired. So, so tired. I could sleep right now. I relax into Cole's arms. I shouldn't relax around them, but I don't care right now. I can't care right now.

Jayden's voice fills the air right by my head. "I'll be your everything, Jo. I'll be the air you fucking breathe. And every time you forget it, I'll remind you of it." His voice lowers, "You can't live without us. We won't let you."

My eyelids flutter shut as I'm wrapped in strong arms.

JAYDEN

11

Jo IS DROPPING OUT. HER ENTIRE BODY SLUMPS, AND IT MAKES me hard. I should fuck her when she's like this.

Cole shuffles her so her head doesn't fall forward. He gives me a look. "I think you took it too far."

I grab the first aid kit. Jo's knees are scraped and bleeding, and her hands are blistered. She looks so beautiful, completely torn apart for us.

"She's fine."

I crack open a water.

Jo's eyes snap open, focusing on the water in my hand. Her entire body locks up. "No! No, no, no."

"Shhhh," Cole tightens his grip. "We have to get you cleaned up."

I splash water over her knees. Jo fights, the clarity in her eyes gone, pure fear taking its place.

"Easy," Cole mutters.

Jo doesn't listen. Or can't. She thrashes her whole body.

"Get my bag," Cole grunts.

Jo looks at me but doesn't see me. It's like she's looking through me.

I watch in fascination. I've seen Jo afraid before, but it's just as intriguing every time it happens. Will I break her this time? What will she do after she breaks? Will she fall apart in my hands and let me hold the pieces?

Doubtful.

Which just means I haven't worked her just right yet.

"Get me a candy."

I glance at Cole.

"A lemon drop." He gestures impatiently.

"You can eat after," I grunt. He's distracting me from Jo's downfall, and it's pissing me off.

"Not for me, asshole. For her."

I chuck Cole's bag at him, thoroughly annoyed that I was pulled out of the moment. Cole shuffles around while trying to hold her still.

"What are you doing?"

"The sour will pull her out of her panic." Cole struggles to hold Jo still but slips a candy between her lips, clamping his hand over her mouth.

It takes Jo a second to register, but when she does, her nostrils flare. Her eyes flash to mine, and she's partially back again. Instead of submission, I see fire in her eyes.

My temper flares. Does she not know what's good for her? I could easily kill her, and yet, she's still poking the bear.

Cole mutters in Jo's ear, "You're going to hold still so we can treat your cuts."

Jo fights, trying again to pull out of Cole's arms.

"No," he winces, a look of vulnerability flashing over his face. "Let me hold you."

I glance at Cole. "Are you hurt?" I check him up and down for injuries.

"No," his face flushes.

I frown. "Why'd you wince?"

"Fuck off." Cole glares at me.

I frown again. Is he upset she's fighting him? Join the fucking club.

I get to treating Jo's knees. There are a few open scrapes, and the rest is just roughed-up skin. The bandage on her arm is soaked and dirty. I pull it off, checking the barely scabbed wounds underneath—the marks of her ownership.

The marks she goaded us into making because she doesn't know when to fucking stop.

"I have more pain meds in my bag," Cole says.

I raise an eyebrow. She doesn't need those. Natural consequences. How else will she learn?

Cole glares at me and fishes in his bag.

"You're getting soft," I mutter.

Cole grabs the pill bottle with one hand. "And you're being a dick. Hand me a water."

Jo immediately panics again.

"Never mind, it's okay. You can take it without."

Cole gives Jo the pills while I clean the cuts on her arm. They look good, still angry and inflamed, but not infected. They'll heal nicely into little pink scars. She'll wear our initials for the rest of her life.

My dick jerks.

I walk around the car to grab my phone so I can take a picture of Jo. As I do, I catch a glimpse of my reflection in the mirror, and for a second, I see Pat's face.

My world grinds to a halt. I stare at my reflection.

He's gone again. It's just me. The same face I've stared at for years.

I squint my eyes, trying to see what it was that made me see him. There's still something wrong with my reflection.

My gut churns. Pat's not here. He's not here—I killed him.

I jab my finger at the reflection in the car. "I killed you, motherfucker."

Familiarity hits me, and I see it. It's the eyes. They look mean and excited. Like he did. Like Pat.

Fear rolls through me, and I slam my fist into the reflection. Once, twice, three times, until pain jabs up my hand and down my arm.

"Jayden?" Cole says.

I step back, gasping for breath.

Fuck. Killing Pat was supposed to make it go away. Supposed to make it all go away.

So why in the hell is he still here?

12

I'm DROWNING AGAIN. WATER SURROUNDS ME. I'M SWIMMING IN *it, and I can't catch a breath.*

I flail my arms, thrashing my way to the top, where my head pops out of the water.

I'm in an indoor pool at a hotel, and my mom is sitting in a lounge chair, texting on her phone.

I look at Mom with yearning.

"Mom?" I rasp.

She waves me off. "Busy, baby."

There's a birthday gift by her feet.

It's my birthday.

I still try to get Mom's attention.

Mom doesn't react. Desperation fills the room, and I splash her.

Mom gasps, instantly snapping at me, "Jesus, Mary. Don't get my fucking phone wet."

I know the answer before I even ask. "Play with me?"

Mom gives dream me a pitying look, and it shoots ice into my gut, but not like I know her next words will. "No." Mom stands. "I hate you, Mary Jo. I wish I never had you."

My world implodes in on me, and suddenly, I'm drowning again. I can't breathe. I can't fucking breathe.

I jerk awake, gasping. Something is squeezing my neck.

"Can't breathe." I claw at my throat.

"Hey," a low male voice says.

I snap my gaze over. Cole is driving, and he reaches his hand and puts it on my thigh. I try to ground myself. I'm in the front seat, not in my nightmare.

"You're okay. It's okay, just focus on me." Cole squeezes once, twice, and looks over at me again.

My gaze darts around the car. "Where are we?"

"You passed out again." Cole looks back at the road, his thumb rubbing circles on my leg. "Somewhere in Oklahoma."

I sit stiffly back against the seat, still feeling like I'm in that hotel pool. The drowning was new for that dream, but everything else was the same. It felt so real.

I check the back seat. Jayden lays stretched out as much as he can, his eyes closed.

More swirling on my thigh. I shove Cole's hand off me. "Don't touch me."

Suddenly, Cole's hand snaps back to my leg, squeezing harder. "Don't tell me what to do, little one."

Rage burns through me. Does he think he can just pretend that nothing happened? Like everything is fine?

I whirl on him. "I'm not your little one; I'm your prisoner. Stop trying to make it seem different."

For a second, Cole doesn't react. Then his gaze slowly turns toward me, and he squeezes hard enough to make my leg hurt. "Is that right?" Anger flashes in his eyes.

"Yes." I grip his hand with both mine and yank. It does nothing except send a bolt of pain through me.

"You're hurting me," I hiss.

Cole immediately loosens his grip. His jaw clenches, and then he slowly lets me go and flexes his hand.

I shove away from him. My dream is fresh in my mind, and everything feels so real and overwhelming. My mom's dismissal of me, their dismissal of me, it all feels like one giant wave that's going to crash over me and drown me in its emotions.

Cole's jaw clenches again.

I want the emotions to stop. I turn to the window. "Why don't you just fucking kill me? Just kill me like you did Sage, and don't drag it out."

"Jo..."

"No," I bite back. Cole's voice is so calm, and that just pisses me off more. How dare he try to be soft after that. *How dare he?*

My eyes burn, and I watch the landscape go by. Giant wind turbines dot the landscape, turning lazily in the bright sun. Why can't they be a little soft? I like their violence, but fuck. Do I?

A single, hot tear runs down my face.

"Lemon drop," Cole tries again.

I ignore him, watching the turbines. Lonely, massive machines. Some of them are broken down and not moving. Carissa told me that people don't tear them down once they break—it's too expensive and dangerous. They just leave them up like a giant graveyard of lonely machines.

Somehow, that makes me even more sad. More tears trace silently down my cheeks, and the back of my throat hurts.

We drive in silence for a long while. Cole tries to talk to me, and I ignore him every time. I refuse to look at him, too. He tries all kinds of tactics to get me to talk.

Finally, he grinds out, "You're being a bit of a bitch right now."

What...did he just say?

Slowly, I turn my head to look at him.

Cole throws me a haughty look. "Oh, there she is. What, just needed a little shit to get you to come out and play?"

"Play?" I raise my voice. I thought I stuffed the emotions down, but they're simmering at the surface. "This isn't some little game, Cole. This is my *life*. You've stolen my life! Kidnapped me and treated me like shit. Worse than shit."

"Would you guys keep it down?" Jayden groans from the backseat.

Cole throws me a look. "You're ours, Jo. We can treat you however we like, and you like it."

I laugh bitterly. "Spoken like a true man. Oblivious. I'll never stop running from you."

Suddenly, Cole swerves the car to the side of the road. I grip the door handle to avoid being slammed into the side of the car.

"What the hell?" Jayden growls.

Cole throws the car in park, jumps out, and rounds the front of it. He bends down for a minute, picking something off the ground. Adrenaline fills me. I'm not sure whether to run or fight, so I tense up and prepare for both.

Cole yanks my door open, and heat rushes into the car. He's holding a handful of flowers from the side of the road.

"Is this what you want, Jo?" Cole cocks his head. "You want a man who will give you flowers? Be home at five every night, ask for sex once a week, and otherwise ignore you?"

I don't take the flowers, and Cole drops them on my lap, putting each hand on either side of me. He leans into my personal space until we're nose to nose. He smells like dirt and spearmint.

"No, I don't think that's what you want at all. I think you like the push and pull. The anger, the hate. I think you love it. I think it makes you feel alive." Cole's blue eyes spark with fire and excitement. He snaps his hand out, grabs the leash attached to the collar, and wraps it around his fist. He yanks me even closer to him, smashing my face into his and putting immediate pressure on my neck. "I think you want to be owned and forced, Jo. I think that's what gets you going. So stop pretending like you don't like it and stop saying that you'll run, 'cause I'll never let you run again."

I come to my senses and shove back against Cole's shoulders. He doesn't move for a second, staring down into my eyes, making sure I know he could keep me here all day. His gaze bounces between my eyes and my mouth. Then, he loosens the pressure on my throat.

I suck in a breath, then shove him again. Adrenaline rushes through me. "Get fucked, Cole. I hate you."

He smirks. "Good. Hate me all you want, baby, but don't you dare ignore me again."

Cole walks around the car and gets back in. He smooths his hair down and looks in the mirror. "Wakey wakey, sunshine."

Jayden huffs. "Want to get off the side of the fucking road and stop drawing attention to us?"

Cole gives a mock salute.

I shove the flowers off my lap.

Cole pulls back onto the highway and keeps driving. The car is silent for a long time. I want to pull the collar off my neck and throw it out the window. To scream that I don't belong to anyone.

Under it all, there's a nagging excitement that I hate. He's paying attention, and I want to think that could last. I really do.

But I refuse to get hurt again.

Cole's voice startles me. "Did you hear me?"

"What?" I glance at him.

"I asked why you go for douchebags?"

I stare at Cole. He grins, and I want to smack him in that pretty mouth.

"You tell me. You're the biggest douche I've ever met."

Cole rolls his eyes. "Please. I've studied the shit out of Kyle," he grinds his teeth together, "and I still don't get it. He did nothing for you, and yet you stayed. Willingly."

I cross my arms as heat flares over my cheeks. "How do you know he did nothing for me?"

"Because I watched you, Jo! What do you think I've been doing these past few months? Before we knew you, you practically lived online, and I spent the last six months living every second with you." Cole grips the steering wheel so hard that his knuckles turn white. "He made your eyes look dead, Jo."

I look away from Cole, defensiveness bubbling under my skin. "Why do you care?"

"Because I do!"

"Well, for starters, Kyle never kidnapped me."

"Sounds boring." Cole smashes the radio on, switching to a rock station, and begins nodding his head to it. "He did kind of look like your dad."

"What?" I sputter. "No the fuck he didn't!"

Cole continues to rock out. "He never gave you any jewelry. Or if he did, you never wore it. Do you like gifts?"

I grit my teeth. "I like silence."

"Not my specialty. Too bad. But I do give some nice gifts. And back rubs." Cole winks at me.

"Sorry," I snap. "I don't accept those as payment for kidnapping and drowning me."

Cole glances to the backseat. "Sounds like you're shit out of luck, Jay. Cross back rubs off your list."

Disbelief runs through me. He's making this all a joke. My life is a fucking joke to him. He's so cocky and self-assured like he's already won me over. "You can't tell me you've kidnapped and tortured your exes like this, and it's worked for you."

As soon as the words come out of my mouth, I freeze. I know exactly how Jayden treated his ex. And I know they mess around together. What if they're serial killers? They grab a girl, mess with her life, fuck her at the same time, then kill her?

Suddenly, I feel sick.

"If you must know, I don't have exes." Cole glances over at me.

I want to swallow, but my mouth is too dry. Because they're dead?

"I don't." Cole shrugs. "No one ever stayed longer than a night."

"They were like a revolving door," Jayden grumbles.

Something in me cringes at that thought. Of course a lot of women wanted Cole. On the outside, he's the ideal man. And for some irrational reason, the thought of a bunch of women fawning over Cole angers me.

Cole winks at me. "I couldn't settle down. The point still stands. Tell me what you want in a relationship because I've never done this shit before."

My mouth dries up. The car goes silent except for the radio.

Did he just imply we were in a relationship? After all of this? This is the farthest fucking thing from a relationship.

I scoff, so angry I can't put anything into words. I look out the window. As we drive, my thoughts bounce between my past relationships, these men, and what I actually want. Fuck, I want a boyfriend who actually cares. I've never been happy in my relationships. Turns out my first boyfriend was gay, and Kyle never cared about me. I just wanted them to care—to pay attention to me.

But I'll be damned if I'll tell Cole that. I will never beg someone to care. Not anymore. I want them to care because they want to, not because I beg them to.

"Jo," Cole's voice is tight. "I asked you a question. What do you want?"

I glance out the window again, saying mockingly, "I want breakfast in bed."

"Okay. What else?"

I roll my eyes. "I want to live close to the grocery store so I can get whatever I want whenever I want. A 24-hour grocery store."

"Okay," Cole says as if that's perfectly reasonable, even though I wasn't being serious.

I laugh. This is the stupidest conversation I've ever had. "I want someone filthy rich so I can travel the world. I don't want to work. I want to eat foods from all over the world while my man waits on me hand and foot." Or men. I could have a harem of them while we're just making shit up.

"That's it?"

I roll my eyes. "And I'd like a unicorn."

"A unicorn I can't do. What about a real animal?"

"Unicorns are real." They are in this fake fantasy we're talking about.

Cole chuckles. "I'll check Amazon for one. In the meantime, what about a dog?"

I sneak a glance at Cole.

"Don't tell me you don't like dogs."

I do. I love them. I've wanted one for forever. I allow myself a shrug. "A dog would be fine." In this imaginary world.

"Good." Cole's hand drops over my thigh, and he grips me. "Believe me or not, Jo, but I want to make you happy."

Instantly, I'm uncomfortable. Cole looks over at me. I refuse to look at him, but I feel his eyes on my face.

"Okay, you don't like emotions. How about this." Cole's voice drops an octave, "You can fight this. Us. But don't try to actually get away. I'd rather kill us both than have you abandon us again."

I freeze. Everything freezes, and I stop breathing.

Cole pulls away, the seriousness in his face dropping away to his happy mask. He winks at me. "Capiche?"

13

Seventeen Years Old

I GRIP the phone so hard I feel the edges cutting into my hand. My knee bounces, and I feel the sweat dripping down my back in this stupid suit.

The phone rings and rings and rings.

Just like I knew it would.

"Fucking hell." I hang up and throw the phone onto the couch.

Jayden's mom walks by.

Immediately, I put on my fake smile, pissed that she saw me like that. She doesn't act like she's noticed. She's getting dressed up for graduation, putting on an earring as she walks. His mom got her life back together after she met Pat. Well, she stopped shooting up with my mom. She definitely doesn't have her life together.

"She didn't answer?" his mom asks.

I clench my jaw and then put on a smile. "It's all good. She's probably busy."

"Oh, honey." The pity that enters her dark eyes makes me sick.

I dart my eyes to my feet, putting on my charming persona that everyone loves. "You look nice today."

She smiles. "My son doesn't graduate high school every day. My *sons*."

Internally, I cringe. I didn't think Jayden or I would make it. Jayden got into fights almost every day. I couldn't because I'd get kicked off the wrestling team, but I wanted to. I helped Jayden a few times when he threw a mask at me and said he needed help. Things with his classes got so bad he got set back a year. I spent most of my time hunting, taking my aggression out in the woods so I wouldn't kill anyone at home.

Neither of us should be here right now. But here we are.

My mom should be here, too. I haven't asked much of her. This'll be the last time I come crawling to her, begging her not to abandon me.

Jayden's mom continues to stand there, her eyes filling with tears. "I'm sorry she isn't here."

"Come here." I open my arms. I try to pretend Mom not being here doesn't hurt—like her not being here for my whole childhood doesn't hurt.

I hate her. I'll never give another woman the power to leave me again.

JAYDEN

14

"What do you think about a dog, Jay?" Cole leans back, acting nonchalant. But I know him. I see the tension in his shoulders.

"We need a place to live to have a dog," I grumble, fishing Jo's phone out of her bag. Hers is the only one we could keep since the cops don't know she has this one. It's how she kept hidden from us for so long.

I open Jo's social media and check the likes on her picture. The post has blown up. There are all kinds of comments, ranging from intrigued to worried to skeptical.

Victory fills me, and I smirk. "Take a look, Jo."

Jo shoots a glare at me but does as I ask. She glances it over. "And?"

"And? And the two posts I made for you have done the best."

Jo snorts and turns away. I see her cheeks getting pink.

A shot of anger runs through me. "Are you embarrassed about us, kitten?"

She shakes her head, but she's stiff. Her discomfort makes my dick spring to life.

I struggle to focus. "Cole. Try calling your mom again." She's the only one who can foot our bill out of the country. I hate the idea of going all the way to Ohio for money, but if we have to, we have to. This isn't the kind of cash I can rob someone on the side of the road for. I need hundreds of thousands.

I reach over to slide my hand down Jo's front.

"Already tried her," Cole says.

Jo tries to squirm away, and I pinch a nipple—hard.

"Fuck!" Jo tries to swat my hand away. "You're such a dick!"

"Fine. I'll call her again."

"No," Cole snaps. "She won't talk to you. You know she hates cops."

"Good thing I'm not a cop." I toss Jo's phone to Cole and reach over Jo's seat.

"Where were we?" I grab the leash in my right hand and slide my left down her torso. "Oh, that's right. You forgot who you belong to."

"Right," Jo grits.

I yank the leash hard. "Already sassing? Damn, kitten must want to be punished."

Jo squirms again. I love it. I'm addicted to the way she responds to us. She's so expressive and hateful and fucking *alive*. She doesn't know when to stop fighting, and I can't take my eyes off her as she burns herself to the ground.

I was alive, too, once.

If I push her, will she also implode like I did? A sick part of me wants to know—wants her to fall over the edge with me.

I see Cole glancing at the phone from the corner of my eye. He has the keypad pulled up, but he isn't dialing.

Internally, I wince. "Give that to me."

"No," he snaps. "I'll do it." His chest heaves. Which makes my chest tighten.

"Jo." I need her to distract Cole. "Be a good girl and put on a show for us." I slide my left hand under her pants.

"Fuck you!" Jo digs her little nails into me, trying to get me off her. My fingers brush over her panties. "Are you already wet for me?"

"Dry as the Sahara, actually," she growls.

I lean over the seat, biting her neck just under her collar, making her gasp. Fuck, if her quick sass doesn't piss me off. It'll only make things worse for her.

Cole glances at us. I ignore him completely, sucking on a mouthful of Jo's skin until she cries out and jerks away. My mouth pops off her, and a beautiful deep red mark is left on her.

Fuck. She looks so beautiful. I dive back in, biting down on the line of muscle leading up to her neck.

"Jayden," she hisses.

I bite harder, and my fingers brush her pussy again. "That's Sir to you. Who owns this pussy, Jo?"

"I do."

A shiver of pleasure runs through me. I bite down on her neck harder while I rub circles on her clit.

I hear Cole make the call and the phone rings. I glance over. He's looking back and forth between us and the road.

Jo moans. I groan and jerk the collar just a bit. "Shhhh. Cole is on the phone. Wouldn't want mommy to hear a moaning little slut in the background, would you?"

"If that's what she calls you, I won't judge." Jo clenches her teeth.

This bitch. I press harder on her clit, feeling her body jerk in response. I bite her again harshly, marking her. Claiming her. I want it to hurt. I want it to hurt, and I want it to break her.

The phone rings and rings.

I glance over. Cole's face is a mixture of arousal and pain. I hate that look. It makes me want to kill his mom for ever making him feel like that.

"What do you think, Cole? Should I let her come?"

A slow smile creeps across his face while the phone goes to voicemail. "I don't know. She hasn't been very good recently, has she?"

"No," I latch onto another part of her neck. Jo loves the pain. I can feel her arousal soaking through her panties.

Goddamn. I'm so hard I feel my dick straining against my pants. I hate that my marks are going to fade. I should tattoo them into her skin. A living patchwork of my slow destruction of Mary Jo Hall.

"How about this," I say. "If your mom picks up, kitten comes. If not, she doesn't."

Cole immediately dials again while watching the road. His pupils are huge when he looks at us as he tracks my hands on Jo's body.

Jo makes a strangled sound. Her neck and shoulders are sweaty, and her hips buck against me.

The phone rings.

And rings.

And rings.

Jo

15

My body is on fire. The mix of pressure on my neck, pain from Jayden's sucking, and pressure on my clit has me a dripping, sweating, scrambled mess.

I want to come, and I hate myself for that. I shouldn't have let Jayden play with me, but the more I fight, the more he gets off.

And if there's one thing I won't do, it's let Jayden win.

Cole's phone goes to voicemail, and Jayden immediately lets off the pressure on my clit.

I sag, sucking in a breath.

"Damn, little one. You look like you want to come." Cole leans over, his voice mockingly soft, "Should I call her again?"

"Fuck you." I hiss in a breath. Cole looks back at the road, then dials again while Jayden starts rubbing my clit and biting down on my shoulder. He bites so hard that I'm sure he breaks the skin, and I struggle to get away.

He doesn't let me, yanking me back by the collar and cutting off my air.

"No," Cole scolds. "Be a good pet and *sit*."

I can't. The sensations that are rushing to my clit, and the pain are mixing in a floaty cloud of sharpness and ecstasy. It all starts to come to a head, and then: "You have reached the voicemail box of—"

Jayden immediately lets off, popping off my shoulder and letting his fingers whisper over my clit.

"No," I whisper, or think, I'm not sure. Both men chuckle.

"Sorry, little one. Nothing I can do." Cole rubs my thigh. "I bet you want it so bad."

I do. They know how to play my body against me, and they do it so damn effortlessly.

Jayden pulls his hand out of my pants and holds it up. "You're wet, poor thing. Maybe we'll reconsider if you beg."

I scrunch my eyes closed, my clit pounding with the need to come. "Fuck no."

Jayden barks a harsh laugh. "You'll stop fighting if you know what's good for you."

"And you'll *keep* fighting if you want to make us happy."

I crack my eyes open. Cole is watching me with a hungry stare. Then, his gaze darts to Jayden's fingers.

"You wondering how she tastes?" Jayden asks.

"I know how she tastes, motherfucker," Cole snaps. "Like goddamn heaven."

"Here." Jayden moves his fingers to Cole's face. "Show her how she tastes."

I watch with rapt attention as Cole grabs Jayden's wrist and pulls him to his mouth. He opens his mouth slowly, glancing between me and the road as he licks Jayden's fingers.

My pussy spasms again. I'm already on the edge of coming.

Cole doesn't take his eyes off me, his pupils blown, as he cleans Jayden's fingers and, finally, gives me a slow grin. "Your torment tastes delicious, lemon drop." He leans back. "What do we do when life gives us lemons, Jayden?"

Jayden rubs his fingers together. "Rub them in cuts."

I shiver.

Cole casts me a crooked grin. "Make lemon drops."

16

We drive for a while longer, and I can't stop shifting. My panties are soaked, I'm hungry, my cuts hurt, and I need to go to the bathroom.

"You that bad off?" Cole chuckles.

"I have to go to the bathroom."

"Okay, I'll pull over." Cole looks around.

"No. I will not be squatting on the side of the road. I want a normal bathroom."

Jayden snorts. "So you can run?"

"Just where do you think I'm going to go?" I sink further into my seat. "I don't even know where we are."

"No."

Embarrassment fills me. I don't want to explain the details to them, but if I don't get out of this car for a minute, I think I'll crawl out of my skin. Plus, I have to take a shit. "I have to go bad. And I need a shower." I haven't bathed since Rosemarry's house, and I've done a lot of running and fucking since then. I feel disgusting.

Cole glances over his shoulder at Jayden. "We do need gas."

A spark of hope runs through me.

"It's the middle of the day."

Cole shrugs. "Easy to blend in with everyone else. No one will notice us if we're just part of the group."

Jayden grunts. "I don't like it."

"I'm hungry," I say. "I want something fresh. Fruit, cheese, something other than fast food."

"Any other requests, princess?"

Yes, I want to come too. But I don't say that.

After a moment's silence, when Jayden probably thinks of every reason to say no, he sighs. "Cole, look for a Loves. Park in the trucker's lot, away from the building."

"Got it."

It takes us about thirty minutes to find one on the side of the interstate. In that time, I shift excitedly. I need to get out of this car more than I need my next breath. I'm so tired, overstimulated, and under-stimulated at the same time.

People! We'll be back around people. My stomach knots in conflict.

Cole drops his hand on my thigh as if he can sense my thoughts. "You thinking about running?"

I freeze.

Cole squeezes—hard. "You're going to stay by my side the whole time. We came this whole way to get you. Don't think for a second that we'll do something stupid like let you get away."

I swallow. Cole's demeanor has changed. He's serious. I throw a glance back at Jayden. He's sitting up straight—alert. When he's sitting up, I remember just how big he is.

Fuck. I clear my throat. "I won't try anything. I just want to go to the bathroom."

We stop to get gas in the front lot. Cole tells me to wait and fills up the car while I gaze at the building. I sit patiently as Cole gets back in and pulls into the backlot. Our SUV feels small compared to the rest of the semis. Cole pulls into one of the long parking spots meant for a truck.

"I'll stay here," Jayden says.

Cole just nods and turns to me. "We're going to take this off. Just for now."

I hold still as Cole takes the collar off. When it's off, I pull in a deep breath of relief. Fuck, I can breathe. Excitement runs through me.

"Wait." Cole gets out and rounds the car. He's being bossy, but I'll accept it if he lets me out. Cole pops open the door with a flourish of his hand. "Let's go."

I don't even argue with him. My bladder hurts. I step out of the car and suck in a breath of fresh air. Fuck, yes!

Cole grabs my hand. I hiss as his hand squeezes a scrape on my palm. He immediately lets go and grabs my wrist instead. He jerks me closer to him. "Don't fuck with me right now, Jo. In and out, then we're leaving."

I let him pull me along. The lot is nothing but asphalt, semis, and oil stains, but it's the most beautiful thing I've seen.

When we walk into the store, the bell dings. It's moderately busy with people getting snacks and taking bathroom breaks before they get back on the road again. It all feels so...normal.

Cole asks something, but I don't hear him. He squeezes my wrist so tight that I snap my gaze to his. He looks pleasant, but I see the glint of warning in his eyes. "Grab what you want."

"Bathroom." My bladder twinges.

"It's in the shower. First, food."

I think about arguing, but I don't. I glance around, orienting myself. I go to the food section, grabbing a fruit container, some nuts, and some yogurt. My mouth waters. It all looks good.

Cole doesn't stop me, so I go to the drinks. My stomach churns at the sight of the waters. I have to use my other hand to grab a juice, and it looks weird with him clinging to me. Cole reluctantly lets go.

"Deodorant." I move to the health section.

"No." Cole herds me toward the counter. "You can use mine."

I look around him. "Toothbrush?"

"You can use mine."

I frown at him. "Gross."

He smirks at me. "I think it's hot."

"Of course you do," I mutter and move with him, grabbing some more snacks off the racks. "Wait! Pain pills." I turn again. My arm is throbbing like a bitch against the groceries piled up in it.

"Have those too, little one. I'll give you another when we get back."

"Fine." I huff. Cole goes to pay for the items, putting on his usual charisma. There's a pretty cashier behind the counter, and immediately, I stiffen. Cole makes easy small talk with her. Nothing about his body language suggests he's flirting, but still, irrational anger fills me.

"Can we get a shower too?" Cole asks, smiling at the cashier. I smile sweetly and stomp on his foot.

The puff of air Cole lets out makes a victorious thrill run through me. He grabs our stuff and chuckles in my ear, "I'm just getting you your shower, lemon drop."

I huff.

"You jealous?"

"No," I scoff.

Cole laughs softly. He herds me toward the bathrooms and showers. "Liar."

Cole opens the shower door with the code on our receipt. I step in, curious. There's a toilet against one wall and a shower beside it.

The door clicks shut behind us.

"Wait." I turn. "There's no stall. Get out."

Cole crosses his arms. "No way."

"Cole!" Seeing the toilet makes me need to go really bad. "I need to go!"

"Then go."

Anger fills me, and I turn and shove him. "There's nowhere for me to go. You have the code. Give me two minutes."

He stares at me.

"Please," I plead, hesitating. My face burns. "I have to take a shit." I want to keep this one piece of me to myself.

Cole's gaze softens. "Okay. Two minutes." He drops the groceries and steps out.

I bolt over in relief and relieve myself.

Once I'm done, I wash my hands and rip into the snacks. Cole steps back into the room. I groan, popping peanuts into my mouth.

Cole strips off his shirt and turns on the water. The sound of it hitting the ground in a wet stream makes me jump.

Water.

Can't breathe.

I suck in a breath. What the fuck is wrong with me? My stomach sours immediately.

Grow up, Jo. It's just a shower.

I glance at the shower. Cole is checking the temp, his upper body completely bare and rippling with muscles. He looks like he did when he hunted me down—dangerous and powerful.

Cole glances at me. "Those good?"

"Fine." I drop the peanuts back into the bag. I can't eat anything else. Cole hums and turns back to the shower, kicking off his shoes.

I won't be able to breathe in there.

My throat tightens at the thought, and panic slams into me. I won't be able to breathe. Pain tightens in my chest. I try to take a deep breath in, but I can't take a full breath.

This is all in my head. It's just a shower. I've showered before.

"Jesus, that's hot." Cole hisses, yanking his hand back out.

I blink slowly, gaze fixed on him.

He did this to me. They did this to me.

Suddenly, I have the urge to run as fast and as far as I can. To get away from the person who's trying to drown me with him.

And he will. I have no doubt he will. It won't be much longer before I'm fully under their control. For fucks sake, they've done all kinds of horrible things to me, and somehow I'm still here?

I take a single step back.

Cole glances at me. "You ready?"

I swallow.

Cole runs his gaze over me, and he immediately stiffens. "Jo..."

I turn and run. If I don't hide, I'll stay. And I'm not sure I'll survive that.

17

I SEE THE INSTANT JO DECIDES TO RUN. HER EYES ARE BOTH vacant and full of fear, and it makes my stomach clench.

Fuck! I throw my shoes back on. "Jo!"

The door swings shut after her. I dart out after her. She's already down the hall, running.

From me. She's running from me.

Fiery anger fills me. I warned her. Told her not to do this. Not right now.

"Jo!"

She darts to the left into the grocery section. I follow after her. I round the corner of an aisle and see her running toward the front door. And then I see something that makes my whole world freeze.

There, at the counter, stands a cop. He watches Jo run, and his gaze bounces from her panicked face to the bandage on her arm.

A bolt of real fear runs through me.

Jo glances over her shoulder at me, then clocks the cop. She immediately slows.

The cop follows her gaze back to me, chasing her shirtless.

I slow my roll, giving him an apologetic smile and a you-know-how-it-is shrug. Then I lock gazes with Jo. "Let's go, babe."

She backs toward one of the doors. Not the one we came in.

Fear fills my veins. I plead with her in my eyes. Don't do this. Don't run from me. Not for real. Don't abandon me.

Jo whirls and bolts out the front door.

My world grinds to a stop.

I can't chase her. Not in front of the cop who's watching both of us. She's a missing person, and I'm wanted for murder.

I can't chase her.

Helplessness washes through me. It cramps my gut. I haven't felt this in years. Stopped feeling it when my mom didn't show up for my graduation. I've avoided it ever since by kicking every girl out immediately after fucking. By making people run from me. Being toxic on purpose so that they run.

I never let anyone get this close. The only exception is Jayden, and he's even more toxic than me. And now the only woman who's managed to weasel her way into my heart is running. And not because I told her to.

Because she doesn't want me.

I move to the back door. As soon as I'm out of the eyesight of the cop, I sprint to the car. Jayden must see me and sits up straight.

I yank the passenger door open, and my crushing realization is summarized in two words: "She's running."

JAYDEN

18

My stomach drops as soon as I see Cole running shirtless without Jo. I immediately focus, and my vision narrows. All that matters is her.

I throw the car into drive. "What happened?"

Cole grits, "There's a cop."

"What the fuck?" My voice drops. "Where?"

"Front lot."

Cole is freaked out—more freaked out than I've seen him in a long time.

I step on the gas, flooring it. We fly into the front lot, and I cuss as people cross the lot right in front of me.

I spot the cop. He's looking across the lot, and I follow his gaze.

Jo looks both ways before running across the busy street to a McDonald's.

I slow enough that I don't draw the cop's attention and drive after Jo. The road is busy, and I have to stop and wait for traffic to clear.

"Fuck. Just go!" Cole shouts.

"Can't." I grit my teeth.

"Jesus." Cole slams his fist onto the dashboard.

"It's okay, we'll get her back." We better. Finally, the traffic clears, and I fly across the road.

I don't see her in the parking lot. She must be in the restaurant.

Or in one of the cars.

My stomach sinks. Finding her will be much harder if she gets in someone's car. I need to grab her before she can do that.

"Park around back. I'm going inside." I throw the car in park and dart out, not bothering to shut the door. I hope she's being rash and is hiding inside. Hiding somewhere I can find her. I rip the door to the restaurant open.

She better hide, and she better hide well. Because I don't think I'll ever stop punishing her for this.

Jo isn't in the lobby. I didn't expect her to be. I stride straight to the bathroom and rip open the door.

A middle-aged woman at the sink looks at me and gasps.

"Get out," I bark, my voice dark. I'm so done with this. The woman leaves, squeezing past me.

Only one stall door is closed, and it's the big one at the back. I stride over to it and boot it open.

There's a resounding crack, and then it explodes open. I'm in before the door has even bounced back.

Jo jumps at me from her spot on the toilet. I barely have time to duck before she's beating on my head.

"Fuck you! Fuck you, Jayden."

I wrap her up and slam her into the wall. "Thought you could run from us, Jo?" She's so small compared to me that I barely feel her attempts to get away. I duck down, putting my shoulder in her stomach, and lift her up.

Jo beats on my back and screams as I march her out of the bathroom. We've already made so much of a scene, but it doesn't matter anymore. We'll throw her in the car and run.

As I stride into the lobby, my gaze locks with the cop from the gas station.

He freezes, seeing Jo fighting on my shoulder, and for a second, I freeze, too.

Fuck.

I whirl before and dart through the kitchen, dodging employees. Someone shouts at me. I ignore all of them and pray that Cole is waiting in the back lot.

"Stop! Police!"

I don't stop. I dart around a fryer and almost slip, headed to the back exit. Jo bounces on my shoulder, and I hold her steady.

"Jayden!"

"Police! Stop!"

Jo screams, burying her head into my shoulder. I slam into the exit door, bursting outside. There! The car is right there. I run up to it, yanking the door open.

"Stop, or I'll shoot!"

Everything slows down. If he shoots me, he'll hit Jo. Suddenly, I'm stuck. I'm stuck like I was on the steps when Pat looked at Cole and made him a target.

I'm staring at the inside of the car, the sounds of the world going fuzzy around me.

Something falls slowly across my vision. I watch it slowly. It's Jo. She's scrambling into the seat.

I cock my head. Why is she going so slow?

"Jay." The voice sounds like it's coming through water.

Pop!

Something loud cracks through the fuzz and explodes to my left.

I blink and look over. There's a hole in the B pillar of the car.

Pop! Pop!

Two more holes appear near my head.

Fuck, he's shooting at us.

My legs feel like they're stuck in mud. I put one in the car. I feel something yanking on my shoulders. I move my other leg inside as Jo looks at me wide-eyed. She's screaming something, but I'm not sure what.

It feels like it takes forever to turn around and pull the door closed. When I do, the car is already flying out of the lot.

Sound comes rushing back. Jo is panting, still holding onto my shoulders. "Fuck! He's shooting! He's shooting!"

"Get the fuck down!" I pounce on Jo, holding my body over her, waiting for the rest of the shots. Nothing comes.

"Are you hurt?" I pull back a little and run my hands up and down Jo's body. My hands shake a little. My heart is racing. I still feel like things are moving so slowly. No blood. I don't feel blood. Why don't I feel blood?

"I'm fine, Jayden." Jo shoves my hands off her.

"Jo!" I grab her chin and force her to look at me. "Are you hurt?" She can't be okay.

Three shots. That's how many I took when I killed that man in the line of duty. Two to the body, one to the head.

"Cole?" I turn to him, looking at his head. It's not covered in blood. I lean over the console, shoving him back against the seat so I can look at his body.

"I'm fine, Jay." Cole weaves in and out of traffic. He glances back at me. "You good?"

I don't believe him. Three shots. Three shots. Back in the day, I was surprised by how little blood there is when someone's freshly shot. Now, I'm not.

I had to have missed something. Someone has to be hurt.

I check over Jo again.

"Fuck, Jayden!" she yells, then hides her head under her arms. "Just leave me alone." Her shoulders shake as she heaves out sobs.

I glance at Cole again. He looks steely. Pissed.

Two to the body. One to the head.

That cop was going to shoot two innocent people. Fuck, how could he have been so stupid?

I sink back into my seat, and it strikes me that I almost lost the only two people I care about in one moment because I froze. Again.

A sick feeling fills me. Every time I care, it ends up hurting the people I love.

And I can't have that. I have to stop fucking caring.

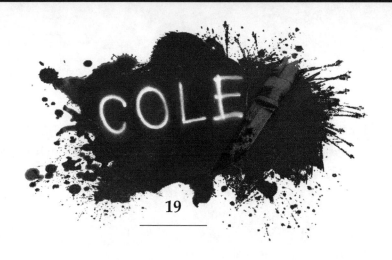

19

I'M FLYING DOWN THE INTERSTATE. THE NEEDLE IS PUSHING 125, and I keep pressing.

"Get off the highway," Jayden demands.

"What?" I barely hear him over the chaos in my head.

"Get off the interstate! Every cop around here will be looking for us, and they'll chase us to the end of the earth on this long open road."

I have to consciously force myself to slow down. I glance back. Jo is crying. Despite my anger, alarm fills me. "Is she okay?"

Jayden checks over her again. "I think so."

"What do you mean, you think so?" Either she is, or she isn't. Anger rushes through me, followed by fear.

She tried to run from us. From *me*. Again.

I slam my hand on the steering wheel, hitting hard enough to hurt. I do it again, hoping it'll ground me.

It doesn't. It's not enough. I need more pain.

We drive for a while—I'm not sure how long—and everything inside me is in turmoil. We only just got Jo back, and it almost happened again.

And it hurts just as much as it did last time.

At some point, Jo falls asleep, and Jayden closes his eyes, but I know he's not sleeping. He keeps checking on me when he thinks I'm not looking.

As the sun goes down, the landscape becomes more wooded.

My leg bounces. I need to park and get out. I need to be alone. Memories and feelings that I try to keep tamped down are creeping up, trying to live in my mind.

Fuck. I need a fucking cigarette. I shake my head. Get it together. You're not like this.

Pat's face sneers across my vision, and I swerve.

Fucking hell. I need to park. And then sleep. How much sleep have I gotten in the last 48 hours? An hour? My head is pounding, and I can't get my leg to stop bouncing.

Finally, I find a spot down a deserted road that we can pull off into. I follow a bumpy path into the woods that looks like it hasn't been driven on in ages, then park. Total darkness falls when I turn the car off, and the lights go out.

I jump out, grabbing my bag. Jayden tries to ask me where I'm going, but I snap that I'm taking a piss and stride into the forest. Once I'm far enough away, I feel like I can take a breath and sink my hand into my bag. I'm shaking, and it's dark and hard to see.

Good boy. You bleed so pretty for me.

Fuck! I shake my head. Fuck, I need sleep.

Want to make your daddy proud? Cry harder for me.

I clench my fist around the knife. My knife. The last thing my mom gave me as a kid before she really spiraled.

I was going to give the knife to Jo before she ran—the first time.

I suck in a sharp breath and flip the blade open. I slide my pants down far enough to expose the top of my thigh, where there's a row of silver lines, some fresher than others.

My hand shakes, and I take a breath to steady it.

As soon as I make the cut, I let out a groan. Fuck. That delicious pain bites into the voices in my head. Stills them. Quiet's them.

I make another cut, this one deeper.

Fuck. My dick flexes, then shame rolls through me.

You gonna come for Daddy while he cuts you?

I grunt, driving the fist wrapped around the knife into a tree, crushing my fingers between the bark and the handle. Pain, beautiful pain, explodes again and drowns out Pat's voice.

I didn't tell Jayden I started cutting again after Jo ran. I thought they would notice in the hotel room, but the light was dim enough, and neither of them said anything.

Blood drips down my leg and cools as the light wind brushes over it.

Jo is afraid of me. She ran again. I didn't keep my promise to make things better.

I reach down, digging my fingers into the cuts, hissing again. I dig until the only thing I can feel is the pain.

Until everything else disappears.

20

I wake with the slamming of the car door. For a minute, I panic. My heart races, and I peel my face off the leather upholstery.

It's dark outside. Cole stalks into the woods, and Jayden gets out of the car. "Stay," he orders, his voice mean.

For once, I listen. What else am I going to do? Run?

My body sags in fatigue. I'm so damn tired. I know I'm going to pay for trying to get away, and Jayden is going to enjoy every second of it. He might even kill me.

Somehow, I'm sure they'll make it hot.

I laugh to myself. Fucking hell, Jo. What the hell is wrong with you? I'm tired. I'm so tired I can't think straight.

I hear Jayden rummaging in the trunk. I glance back, and he slams the trunk down, then stares at me through the glass. His eyes are wild and unhinged—animalistic.

I freeze.

Jayden continues to stare with an odd look on his face. It's like he's looking through me.

My heart starts racing again. I shift.

Jayden's eyes don't follow me.

Is he...? I watch him. Is he looking at himself in the window?

Jayden stands there frozen. Finally, he shakes himself out of it and moves to my side of the car.

I scoot as far back as I can.

Jayden opens the door, taking in my pitiful attempt to get away. Instead of victory, I see an odd mix of conflicted emotions in his eyes. "Come here, Jo."

I shake my head.

A flare of heat fills his eyes before he squashes it again. "Now is not the time. Let me see your arm."

I hesitate.

"Kitten. Now."

I swallow. Where am I going to go? I sag in defeat and scoot over to him. Jayden grabs my arm in his warm hands, gently turning it over so he can see the bandage.

"It's fine," I say, trying to pull my arm out of his hand.

Jayden doesn't even acknowledge me; he just tightens his hold and carefully peels the bandage off.

The skin is all red and scabbed and irritated under it. Some of the scabs opened during my fight with Jayden. I cringe. It hurts like a bitch.

Jayden shakes his head and grabs a first aid kit from his backpack. He grabs the antiseptic and catches my gaze. "Gonna hurt."

I clench my jaw. Jayden sprays it on, and it does hurt. The pain bites through me, waking me up. Jayden continues to clean it up more gently than I expected, then layers on a clean bandage. He tapes it to my arm, then reaches for my knees. He checks the minor cuts there, then smooths his thumbs over my clammy palms.

I try to pull them away, but Jayden doesn't let me. My palms have no open cuts, just scratches and sore parts.

Jayden presses his thumb into one of the red spots on my palm, looking up at me while I wince. He presses harder, watching me without blinking, his pupils widening. Then he brings my hand to his mouth and kisses it lightly. He bites once, then lets me go and reaches to the front seat, grabbing the collar.

"No," I stiffen.

Jayden ignores me, slipping it around my neck. The cool metal settles on my skin, and immediately, I hate it. I feel trapped. Suffocated. Like I can't breathe.

Jayden digs in his bags and brings out ropes. Thin, blue, red, and purple ropes that look soft.

"What is that?"

"We need to sleep. I don't trust you not to run." Jayden pulls out the red rope.

"What?"

Jayden reaches for my hand.

I pull away.

"Jo," Jayden looks into my eyes. "If you fight me, I won't be able to do it right, and you'll be uncomfortable for the rest of the night."

I freeze.

Jayden cocks his head like he's trying to figure me out. I see the darkness lurking behind his eyes, battling to get out. But for some reason, he's holding back.

I can't tell if that's good or bad.

Finally, I relax. Jayden's eyes lighten with interest, and he traces the rope around my wrist, looping it gently but securely. He wraps the rope around my hips, doing the same to my other wrist, being careful not to run them over my bandage. He ties my wrists to the sides of my waist, working with flow and familiarity—like he's done it a hundred times before.

"Too tight on your waist?"

I shake my head. It's pretty loose.

Jayden puts his fingers in between the rope and my body. "It's going to get tighter, so tell me now if it's bothering you."

"It's not." I narrow my eyes. Doesn't he want me to be uncomfortable? Isn't that his whole life's purpose?

Jayden just goes back to wrapping until my wrists are securely pinned on each side of my hips. Jayden then traces the rope down my front and between my legs.

"What—"

"Tell me if this is too tight." Jayden secures it on the other end. The rope presses against the seam of my shorts, sending a thrill through my clit. I shift to try to alleviate it. "It's tight."

"It's supposed to rub. That's the point. But if it's pinching, that's a problem." Jayden runs his fingers between the rope and my body.

It doesn't pinch. Just puts a constant pressure on my clit.

The door behind me yanks open, and I jump and whirl as best as I can.

"What we doing?" Cole slides in, looking me up and down, hunger flaring in his eyes. "Oh. Damn."

Despite the dim light from the pilot light, I can see the manic glint in Cole's eyes. Cole runs his finger along the ropes. "All trussed up so you can't run from us."

Before I can react, he grabs my hips and swings me toward him. "I'm borrowing her, Jay. I need her."

Cole doesn't look like he normally does. He looks wild and desperate. It sparks fear in me and also makes my clit pulsate. Despite my exhaustion, I start to feel alive again.

Jayden groans, "Don't get my rope dirty."

Cole grins up at me, a wild look in his eyes. "No promises." He leans in, smelling of sweat and *him*. He grabs the rope above my crotch and gently yanks. Pleasure shoots through my clit immediately.

Cole grins, his white teeth flashing, making me want to press my lips to his and bite him. To stain those lips red for what he dared to do to me.

"Fuck, Jo." Cole shoves me down, my head hitting Jayden's lap. He's on top of me in a second, taking my bottom lip in his teeth and pulling.

I try to reach for him, but my hands are securely trapped to my hips.

I moan as Cole pulls my lip hard enough it hurts.

He chuckles.

"Fuck you," I moan.

Cole winks at me, sitting back and flashing his knife. "These shorts are gonna get in my way."

"My rope," Jayden warns.

"I won't touch your fucking rope." Cole shimmies the rope off my pussy and puts his knife there instead.

I freeze, the blade so damn close to my clit. Cole hovers there, watching my reaction.

"You like this," he states.

"No." Energy buzzes through me.

Cole presses the blunt edge into my clit. "Yes, you do, I remember." He snaps his gaze up to mine, and suddenly, he's angry. "I remember everything, Jo."

He grips my shorts, and in a flash, he rips his knife through them.

"Cole!" I gasp, struggling to get away. But I'm trapped. My arms are tied, and he's got my hips between his thighs.

He rips my shorts and panties away from my crotch, exposing my pussy to him.

"I remember your chicken and sage dinners, your favorite cereal, and I remember the tank tops you wore every day."

Cole buries his head in my pussy, taking a long lick. "I

remember your onion powder, your wooden ice cream bowl, and your fucking midol."

Cole bites my clit, making me jump. "I spent months trying to remake the meals you made for us. Also spent months stalking you online. Learning about you. Your family."

He looks at me with an angry glare, yanking his dick out and rubbing it on my clit. I'm already wet, and he knows it. He gives me a devilish smirk.

"I don't think you forgot about us, either." Cole lines up with my pussy and slams inside.

I cry out as he fills me all the way up. Cole yanks back and slams in again, throwing his head back.

"Yeah," I grit, pinned under him. "I remember you guys. What you did. What you put me through."

"Yeah?" Cole reaches down, pinching my nipple hard. "Do you remember all the times you came? Because I fucking do."

I feel Jayden shift under me and stroking himself.

Cole hisses, "Now, you're going to be a good girl and get me off. I'm going to use this pretty little body to come—whether you want me to or not. Got that, lemon drop?"

A rush of heat runs through me.

"Yeah, I think you got that." Cole gives me a sinister smile. "And I'm going to do it over and over until you learn you can't run from us. Ever. I'll fuck you senseless until you get that through your pretty, stubborn little head." Cole's eyes flash in anger, and he leans in. "You don't *get* to say no. You don't *get* to call the shots. We do. We'll take care of you. We'll fight your battles. We'll feed you, clothe you, bathe you, fucking hell, breathe for you. Stop fighting us."

I stare into Cole's eyes. He looks mean. Angry. Oppressive. It makes me want to fight him. To push back against the pleasure he's giving me. I give him a sweet smile. "I'll never stop fighting you."

Cole yanks almost all the way out and slams into me hard.

"Fuck, Jo. I'll reverse this vasectomy and pump you so full of my cum that I'll put another baby in this belly. Then you can never leave me."

I suck in a gasp, pain filling my chest. Our baby.

Everyone in the car stills.

Cole leans over me, his voice cracked, eyes still wild. "I wanted that baby, Jo. I didn't care if it was Jayden's or mine; it was *ours*, and I wanted it. I've spent the last six months missing someone I never knew."

It feels like my chest cracks open. I spent the past six months trying to forget. I wasn't ready. But damn, if I didn't try to hide from myself every time I thought about it.

Cole clears his throat and presses into me again. He reaches his hand down to play with my clit. "Now you're going to come like the dirty slut that you are, and I'm going to fill you so full that my DNA drips out of you every time you move," Cole growls in a possessive tone, and the words send a thrill through me. "I might not be able to get you pregnant now, but I will. Soon. And then you can never leave."

Despite everything, my body loves what he does to me. The way he plays with me numbs every other thought. He builds me higher and higher until I come all over his fingers and dick.

Cole groans, pumping into me steadily. "You're not done yet."

He continues to play with me as I come down, building me back up immediately.

"Cole," I moan, the stimulation heavy and overwhelming.

"Too bad, Jo." He continues playing. "If I have to suffer, you do too. We're in this together."

I jerk away from the restraints, but my hands are securely pinned to my hips. Sensation and pleasure mount until I'm on the edge of coming again.

Cole forces me to come over and over until it begins to hurt. He's angry, and it hurts something deep in my soul.

"Cole, please," I moan.

"Are you begging, Jo?" Cole leans over me, dropping his forehead to mine and tilting his head. I immediately stiffen.

"What are you begging for?"

I clench my jaw.

"Tell me," Cole whispers.

"I'll never beg."

But for the first time, part of me wants to. I want to say that I didn't mean to hurt him. That I'm just exhausted. That I'm tired of fighting to not get hurt.

Cole watches my face. Something like pain flashes across his eyes. "Still hiding from me, I see."

Cole yanks out of me, still hard, and tucks himself back into his pants.

"Don't hide, Jo. Cause I'm going to force every little secret out of that pretty little head, no matter how much I have to hurt you to get them."

Cole slides back on the seat and then opens the door. "Take the collar off, Jay. She can't sleep with it on."

Then Cole steps out of the car and slams the door.

JAYDEN

21

ONE YEAR AGO

"WHAT THE FUCK?" Cole sucks in a breath, seeing Pat trussed up and tied to a chair in the garage. I told Cole I wanted to use his cabin for a few days, but not for this. I park and glance over at Cole. I've been torturing Pat for the past few days, but it hasn't been enough. It'll never be enough.

"Jayden?" For a second, anguish flashes in Cole's eyes as he looks at Pat, sitting bound and gagged, naked in the cold.

Pain runs through me again. I could have prevented this anguish. If only I had done more as a kid. If only I didn't lock up like a stone as soon as I saw Pat's eyes drift over Cole. I did what I thought was enough, but it wasn't. I thought this could make up for it. But clearly, it's just hurting him again.

"Sorry, you can go. I'll kill him today, and it'll be over."

"Jayden." Cole's eyes are locked on Pat. "I think you've lost it."

I wince.

A smile curves across Cole's face.

"We can go."

"No." Cole slips out of the car and slams the door. I follow. Within the last year, I've killed someone on the job, quit that job, and dumped my long-time girlfriend. I'm sure some would say that I've lost it. But I think I've just started living.

Cole strides into the garage, as usual, unafraid to commit. Cole circles Pat, eyeing him up and down. I've tried to keep the injuries insignificant. He has no more fingernails or toenails. I ate a few in front of him before he passed out.

"Hey there, stepdaddy," Cole laughs. "Looking cold. Jayden been treating you well?"

Pat moans. Cole stalks around him, grinning. He looks angry and alive.

For a second, I feel lighter. Cole is happy. I gave him this. The happiness doesn't last long, though.

Cole spends a few hours with Pat. He cuts his eyelids, foreskin, lips, and asshole off, using that pearl-handled knife he's so fond of. Cole stops every time Pat passes out and only starts again when he's back. He doesn't hesitate at all. In fact, he's a bit manic about it.

The more angry Cole gets, the more crippling guilt I feel. My best friend is here, and he shouldn't be. And it's all because of me.

I'll never be able to make this up to him, even if I spend my whole life trying.

JAYDEN

22

MY GAZE LOCKS on Cole's thigh as he leaves the car. There's a dark patch, and it looks like...blood. Warning bells immediately ring in my head. He's hurt. Why didn't he say anything?

I quickly finish my ties on Jo, making sure nothing is too tight. The rope between her legs now sits on her bare pussy, thanks to Cole's work. I secure Jo to the car so she can't run anymore and take off after Cole.

I find him pacing in the darkness, about ten feet from the car.

"Leave me alone, Jayden." Cole waves me off.

I move to see his leg. "You're hurt." There isn't a lot of blood, but it's enough. Did he get shot and not tell me when the cop fired rounds?

"I'm fine."

"No, you're not." I grip Cole's shoulder and whirl him around to face me. His eyes are wild.

"Jay! I swear if you don't fuck all the way off!" Cole jerks out of my grip and turns as if he's trying to hide something from me.

"What in the fuck is going on, Cole?"

Cole runs both hands through his hair, making it stand straight up. He laughs maniacally. Real fear floods me.

Something is wrong.

Cole looks around like he's looking for routes to run from me.

I dart forward, slamming Cole back into a tree.

"What the fuck?"

I ignore him. He got hurt, and he didn't tell me. I grip his pants and rip them down to see the injury. Cole throws me off in a second, but it's all I need.

There are two deep, clean cuts on the top of his thigh.

My world slows down. That's not a gunshot wound. It looks like slices.

Oh fuck. Is Cole cutting himself? Again?

"Don't give me that look, Jay."

I snap my gaze up to his. "What are you doing, Cole?"

He yanks his pants up, and his eyes narrow on mine. "Don't judge me. We all deal with things differently."

"Things?" Failure and anger course through me. I've tried so hard to protect him. Spent my senior year fighting anyone who looked at him wrong and almost got expelled for it. Now, I brought this woman into his life who has wrecked him more than I've ever seen anyone wreck him.

"None of your business, Jayden," he snaps. "I'm not a kid anymore; you don't have to look after me like one."

Rage clouds my vision. I won't let him self-destruct like this. "Give me the damn knife."

"Fuck you." Cole laughs. It's unhinged. This isn't Cole. I've never seen him this unraveled. Except when we were kids. Except for with Pat.

A sharp pain travels through my chest. I have to deal with this.

I take a step toward Cole. "If you don't give the knife to me, I'll take it from you."

Cole takes a step back, laughing bitterly. "Like I said, fuck you, Jayden."

I eye him. He doesn't know what's good for him. He needs sleep. How long has he been awake? At least a day and a half, minus a small nap.

Cole moves with me every time I move, watching me closely, muscles tense.

He can't make good decisions, so I'll make them for him. "Don't make me fight you, Cole. You're not in your right mind."

Cole spits onto the ground. "Just because I cut doesn't make me crazy, Jayden. Stop being a fucking cunt."

If he won't take care of himself, I'll do it for him. I walk calmly toward him. I act confident, but I'm not. I spent high school fighting, but Cole spent it wrestling. I know the only way I can win this is if I fight dirty. And I don't want to hurt him.

"I'll give it back once you've had some sleep." I won't.

Cole shakes his head.

There's a slight noise from the car, and Cole turns slightly to glance at it.

I strike. I throw a quick, light blow to his head. Cole doesn't duck in time, and it glances off the side of his face. I sweep his legs out from under him, and I'm on top of him in a flash.

"Jesus," Cole immediately closes the distance between us, gripping one of my arms to flip us. I swoop my arm out of his hold, but he has my opposite leg wrapped just as quickly. Cole bucks both of us up, and before I realize it, my other arm is trapped under his, and he's flipping us so I'm underneath him. Cole presses all his weight into me, pinning me to the hard ground. I try to free my hand to reach into his pocket to get the knife.

"By all means, keep fighting me, Jayden." Cole sounds bored. "It hurts. I like it."

I stop.

Cole shakes his head in disgust. "You're fucked up, you know that? Stop trying to help me and focus on yourself."

I grit my teeth. I don't matter.

"See? That right there." Cole pushes off me, dusting off his hands and standing. "You can't make up for the past, Jayden."

I push up, glaring at him.

Cole gives me a frustrated look. "Pat got me too, Jay. I had a shitty mom. That's my burden to bear. I'm sorry, but stop trying to fix me." He turns around and stalks back to the car.

Fuck. The words hit me in the chest. We've only openly talked about it once. The day he told me about it at the beginning of my senior year. It rips open an old scab between us.

I watch Cole yank the car door open and climb in.

Feelings. Too many feelings swirl in my head.

I don't need to fix myself. I just need to stop feeling. That will fix everything. The more I feel, the more the people I care about get hurt. And I can't have that.

I can't feel. I can't be soft.

I'M NOT SURE HOW LONG WE SLEEP. I WAKE UP MULTIPLE times with Cole curled around me in some position or another. If I could have tossed and turned, I would have, but the ropes, his heavy weight, and the small seats made that impossible. Despite that, the ropes weren't uncomfortable, and Cole made sure to take the collar off before I slept, which I appreciated more than I'd tell him.

When we get up, it's getting dark again. They untie me, and I shake the stiffness out of my limbs. I have to change into my last pair of shorts since Cole ruined my other one, and they make me take a piss outside. The whole time, both men are stiff and silent. They're like a storm waiting to happen.

I'm hungry and thirsty, but I don't want to break the stifling silence. No one speaks. Jayden dresses my arm again, and Cole continues to send me obsessive looks. It makes goosebumps prickle across my skin.

When we get back in the car, Jayden gets in the front seat. "Hand me the damn bag."

Cole has slid in next to me, and he slowly cocks his head, flipping his knife back and forth, back and forth.

"For fuck's sake." Jayden shuffles his huge body around and snatches at a backpack by my feet.

Cole kicks it away with his foot. "Why don't you learn to ask for help nicely instead of just strongarming your way through everything."

Jayden stiffens.

The energy rolling around in the car makes the hair on my arms stand on end.

At the wrong moment, my stomach growls. It sounds loud in the silence.

Cole slowly tilts his head toward me. "Are you hungry, little one?"

I swallow. Fuck. I'm not sure what he and Jayden are fighting about, but suddenly, Cole looks at me like I'm the only one on his radar.

Cole gives me a slow, mean smile. "Did I not tell you we'd take care of you?"

I clench my jaw. He waits for an answer.

"Yes," I grind out.

"Then why," Cole leans in, "didn't you tell us you were hungry?"

I glare at him. "I was going to get it myself. Do I have to ask for water and snacks like a damn kid?"

Jayden snorts. I glance at him, and he quickly hides a smirk.

"Oh?" Cole leans back, glancing between the two of us. "You know Jo, you have a lot in common with Jay here. Can't ask for help to save your life."

I don't know what to say to that.

Cole twirls the knife again, and it slips, slicing into one of his fingers. He hisses.

Oh shit, he cut himself.

Jayden whirls around. "Give me the goddamn knife, Cole!"

"Take it from me." Cole winks, throwing his finger in his mouth.

Jayden looks like he's going to lunge into the backseat.

"I'll tell you what." Cole hands me the knife. "We'll play a game for it. Whoever catches her gets it."

I stare at the blade in my hand. This is the same knife I whittled with in the cabin. The same one I fought him with when he chased me and then fucked me within an inch of my life.

Jayden lunges for me, and instinctively, I close my hand around the handle and recoil in the seat.

"Jo," Jayden growls. "Give it to me." His big body is pinned between the two front seats.

The tiny bit of control that I have flows through me.

Cole digs around in his bag and throws something at Jayden. "Gotta wear a mask. Makes it more fun."

"I'm not doing that shit. Give me the knife, Jo."

"If you don't wear it, the deal is off. What, afraid you can't catch her?" Cole gives me a predatory look. "Better run, Jo."

"Don't," Jayden growls.

If I don't get out of here, something is going to happen to me. The pressure is far too high.

I dart out of the car and take off into the woods. The sun is just setting, casting golden light all over the trees and bushes. I run as fast as I can go, tree branches and shrubs whipping my face. A burst of excitement rushes through me, and I feel alive.

I can breathe again. The stifling pressure in the car is gone.

There's a whoop behind me and heavy footsteps. I dart to the right, away from the sound.

Fuck, they're chasing me. The woods are thick with summer growth, which makes running hard.

I need to find somewhere to hide. I scramble down a hill, getting caught by bushes. They claw at and catch on my clothes.

I jump over a small overhang and land heavily on the ground. I roll, then realize the overhang is just enough for me to squeeze under. I scramble under it, breathing heavily.

"Where are you, little one? Don't you want to get caught?" It's Cole's voice, and he doesn't even sound out of breath. Movement catches my eye, and I suck in a breath.

One of them stalks through the woods. He has a ski mask on.

"Here kitty kitty."

It's Cole. I can tell by the voice.

He whirls slowly, scanning the area. I freeze completely.

Cole's blue eyes lock on mine, and a grin stretches across his face. "Oh, hello."

He's about five feet away. I scramble out of my hiding spot and sprint as fast as I can.

"I think she wants to be caught," I hear Jayden say.

I let out a scream. I see Jayden running toward me on the left. He also has a ski mask on.

I dart away. Fuck! They're so damn close. I know I can't outrun them, and I can't hide from them. And that makes a thrill run through me.

I whirl, holding my knife out in front of me, gasping for breath.

Both men slow.

"What a good girl. Running as soon as I told you to." I recognize the voice as Cole, even though they look almost identical in the masks. Cole doesn't even sound out of breath. "I say jump, and you say: how high?"

"Fuck you," I pant for breath. I can only see slivers of their faces. I think Jayden is on the right, and his dark eyes flash with menace.

"Don't come any closer." I slash the blade out at Jayden as he tries to edge up behind me.

"You keep telling us what to do, and you won't be coming for a long, long time."

"Tell us what to do, lemon drop," Cole says. "It makes it all the more fun to punish you."

"Would you stop telling her to do the opposite of what I say?" Jayden snaps.

"Why? It's so much fun."

Both men close in on either side. I maneuver so my back is to a tree so they can't sneak up behind me. I see Jayden throw Cole a nasty glare.

When I glance at Cole to see his reaction, Jayden lunges at me. I snap the knife out, but he darts to the side, batting my arm down. I try to swing it back up, but Jayden is on top of me, shoving me into the tree.

I hit it so hard that the breath explodes from my lungs. Jayden is on me in a second, pressing into me and ripping the knife from my hand.

"Fuck." I jerk my knee up. Jayden doesn't move in time, and I graze him.

"Jesus," Jayden doubles over, and I scramble away.

"Uh uh." There's a hand in my hair and a sharp yank downward that makes me cry out. Cole has stepped between us, pulling me by my hair as he grabs at Jayden. "You've had your fun; now it's time for us to have ours."

I scratch at his hands, but Cole yanks me to the ground, pulling hard enough that my eyes fill with tears. "Atta girl. Get on your knees for us. Submit like the good little whore we know you are."

I blink away the tears, seeing the dirt and leaves where Cole holds me.

"Give it," Jayden gasps to Cole. I hear him pull in a breath through the mask.

"No, no. I'm not done playing." Cole shoves me down, and I catch myself on my hands.

I turn on my knees to face them. Both stand over me, their masks menacing and dark.

"I'm going to give you one chance to take your clothes off, little one." Cole flips the knife in his hand. "And if you don't take that chance, I will cut them off. I know you only have one pair of shorts left."

I swallow. He has me, and he knows it. Despite myself, my pussy pulses. I glare at them and hook my fingers in my pants.

Cole fixes his gaze on me. "Say: thank you, master, for letting me undress for you."

I narrow my eyes further.

Cole cocks his head, and his voice gets lower, "Say it, Jo."

"Thank. You." I grit my teeth.

"Thank you, who?"

If I could reach him to hit him, I would. I bite out, "Thank you, *master*, for letting me keep my clothes." I lower my voice as I yank my pants down and mutter, "Dick."

"What was that?" Jayden is on me in a flash, hand around my throat, forcing my head up to look at him. His eyes narrow behind the mask. "What did you say?"

"Thank you." I narrow my eyes at Jayden further, but I can feel my pulse pick up under his fingers.

Jayden leans down, the fabric of his mask brushing my nose as he squeezes my neck. "So you think you can just disrespect him 'cause we're fighting?" He chuckles, rubbing the fabric of his mask against my neck. "What a silly kitten. Now get your fucking pants off, and we'll see how much you're going to pay for that little comment."

He lets go of me. Heat throbs in my pussy. I yank my pants as far as I can get them while still kneeling. That dark look is back in Jayden's eyes. I see him smirk under his mask, and then he steps behind me. Suddenly, Jayden yanks my shirt over my head, pulling my arms up with it. I try to wiggle out, but I'm yanked back by my shoulders. I cry out as I fall back, unable to catch myself.

My head lands on Jayden. The shirt is over my eyes, and I

struggle to yank it all the way off. Panic rolls through me. The last time they covered my head, they drowned me.

"No, no." Hands land on my arms and pin them above my head. "You don't deserve to see. Right now, I want to hear your pitiful little cries as Cole teaches you a lesson."

I wiggle and arch my back, but a hot hand lands on my hip, holding me down. "Ohhh, Jo. You're wet already. So eager to take our dicks?" There's a tsk. "How embarrassing. I thought you hated us and wanted to run?"

"I do," I suck in a breath. Will this be my last one? Will they drown me again?

"So fucking wet." A finger swipes at my pussy, and I jump at the contact. Fingers land on my clit and rub slowly. "Such a fucking slut for me. That's it. Take it like my good little girl."

I struggle to get away, throwing my head back and forth.

Jayden laughs cruelly. "What is it, kitten? Are you afraid?"

I jump at the snap of a stick. Did they bring water with them? I don't think they did.

There's an intake of breath by my left ear. Jayden chuckles. "You *are* afraid. You talk a big talk, but as soon as we get you in our hands, you crumble. Pitiful."

Pleasure is starting to build in my clit. I start to fight for an entirely different reason.

Cole's fingers disappear. I tense.

Something hard and blunt presses against my entrance. Something foreign.

"Cole!" I struggle.

"Easy now. It's just a knife. Not even as big as the spice jar."

The object is pressed harder into me. I feel it push inside me, all hard edges and cold.

"Wait!" I whip my head back and forth again.

"That's it," Jayden leans into my ear again. "Fucking beg. Fucking beg for mercy."

The handle slips in, rough and harsh. Bites of pain course through me, and I suck in a hot breath against the shirt. I clench down, and Cole's fingers are on my clit again, rubbing circles.

"It hurts," I gasp.

Suddenly, the shirt is ripped off my head, and Jayden's masked face is there, leaning down. His eyes are dark and wild. "I want to see those pretty little tears when you break for me. Go on. Cry. It makes me come."

Cole gently pumps the knife handle in and out of me, pushing up so it grazes my G-spot, and I gasp in pain and pleasure.

I can't handle what these men are doing to me. The constant swing from fear to hate to exhaustion has me strung out on every emotion possible.

Jayden still has my arms pinned above my head, and he moves his hand until it's over my bandage. He squeezes, causing another bolt of pain to run through me. I gasp and arch my back, tears immediately filling my eyes.

Jayden bucks his hips up into me and groans.

Pleasure in my clit builds as Cole continues his assault. Their angry, dominating touch fills me with need, and I clench around the knife handle.

"Good girl. Be a nasty thing, and come on my knife."

I think I'm going to. Jayden gives another harsh press to my cuts.

I squeeze my eyes shut.

"Open, Jo. I want to see you fall apart," Jayden demands.

Cole slows his pace, dropping me from the edge. I snap my eyes open. He winks at me. "Obey him, and you can come."

I drop my head back but keep them open, staring up into the twilight.

Cole builds me back up instantly, and Jayden squeezes my wound. He growls, "You're going to stop running from Cole unless he tells you to. Got it?"

I clench my jaw.

Jayden drops his head to mine, speaking so low into my ear I almost can't hear him, "He trusted you. Then you ran." Jayden jerks his hips up into me. "He spent everything he had to find you, and you ran again. And *again*." Jayden digs his fingers into me and speaks a little louder, "So why don't you stop being a fucking ungrateful slut and stop. Fucking. Fighting."

The adrenaline and dopamine swirl in my head immediately, and a pang runs through my heart. Guilt eats at me.

Cole leans over, lifts his mask up, and spits on my clit, rubbing it in with his fingers.

"Now, come," Jayden demands.

The orgasm rolls over me. Pleasure explodes, and I clench around the knife handle. I come with such intensity that my entire body locks up.

Cole jerks his dick out of his pants and rubs one out over me. He comes with a growl, shooting pearls of cum onto my skin.

"Good." Jayden gets out from under me. He leans over me, and Cole snaps his hand down to the knife handle that's still in my pussy, keeping it from Jayden. He works it out gently, reclaiming it.

"Now that that's handled. We have a situation to take care of."

24

For the rest of the trip, we all reach an unspoken truce. Jo stops trying to run every time we turn our backs, Jayden lightens up on his asshole behavior, and I stop needling everyone every chance I get.

But the closer we get to my mom's house, the more antsy I become. I'm about to see my mom. I've avoided seeing or talking to her for so long. There are too many painful memories that I don't want to relive.

On top of that building dread, I feel like every other driver is looking at our car. Jayden insists no one is paying attention to news from another state, but I know he's just trying to make me feel better. Jo is big news. I don't even have to read the news to know she's all over the headlines.

"Girl who disappeared for months is back and forced into a car with two men accused of murder."

We did another plate switch, this time with a car that didn't even match. But beggars can't be choosers.

We arrive in my mom's area in the evening. She lives about an hour away from the cabin with Ralph. I insisted on driving all day today, but it doesn't help. My legs are jittery, and Jayden keeps looking at the speedometer. I force myself to slow down.

"So, Cole." Jo's in the backseat alone, but she scoots up behind me. "What can I expect from your family?"

"Ralph's not my family," I bite. Anger and adrenaline start mixing inside me.

Jo winces and sits back. Instantly, I feel bad. I'm not sure what to say to fix it. Ralph's not family, and he never will be. Mom isn't much better.

Jayden and Jo are silent for the rest of the drive. Mom moved in with Ralph a long time ago, but they just got married a few months ago.

My chest tightens as I pull down the last street before their house. By the time I hit the brakes to stop in front of the house, I can barely breathe. Ralph is rich as fuck, and the house is a statement. It's two stories tall and has fancy exterior lights and landscaped trees and bushes. It's way bigger than two people could ever need. I've never been inside. I just dropped Mom off once when she relapsed and was too drunk to drive.

I should never have picked her up. Moment of weakness.

But now I'm back—to beg for money.

Jayden unstraps his seatbelt, and the sickening feeling in my stomach almost makes me throw up. This is real. This is happening.

Jayden gets out and rounds the car. He gets Jo out and then taps on the glass.

I can do this. It'll be fine. I unstrap my seatbelt and step out of the car, but as I do so, it keeps moving.

"Put it in park!" Jayden snaps.

Fuck. I jump back in, throw the car in park, then pull in as much of a breath as possible.

I don't look at Jayden. He knows me better than anyone else, and I don't want to see the pitying look in his eyes. Don't want him to see me in this weak moment.

I straighten. We'll just get everything transferred and go. Jayden has a plan to hop on the dark web and pay someone in Bitcoin to get us out of the country. He says it'll be fast.

I rip myself out of my fog and stalk up to the front door. It's big and fancy, covered in ornate carvings. I knock harshly. After a minute, the door opens, and the one person who fills me with dread stands right in front of me.

I snap my mouth shut.

"Cole!" Mom gasps. I notice how much older she looks. She still has bleached blonde hair, but her tattoos are faded and blown out now.

Mom collects herself. "What are you doing here?" Her tone is cold. She still hasn't opened the door all the way.

I throw on my practiced smile. "Hey, Mom."

"What do you want?"

"Ouch. Harsh. Not even a: hey, son! Missed you." I lean against the doorframe, and Mom shrinks back the tiniest bit. It makes me want to laugh as the back of my throat tightens.

Mom still won't look at me. "Murderers aren't welcome in my home, Cole."

There's silence. I feel Jayden's anger at my back.

I smile. "Is Ralph home?"

"Hey Mom, who is that?" a young voice asks.

I blink.

Mom flinches. "I'll be right there."

"Mom?" the voice says.

My ears start ringing. The voice sounds like a young child. Who the hell is calling her mom? I don't have any siblings.

"Who is that?" I breathe.

A little head pops up under my mom's arm. A boy, probably eight or nine, with brown hair and dimples, smiles up at me. "Oh, hey!"

"Cole, this is Sam." Mom's mouth is tight.

"Who is Sam?" I grit.

"He's our son. We're adopting him."

My ears start ringing. Son? Their fucking son?

I'm her son.

I take a step back. The world sounds fuzzy. Now I notice the blue and red kids' shoes by the front door.

I take another step back. I see Mom's mouth moving, but I don't know what she's saying.

My mom replaced me. Just like that.

25

I COULD GUT THIS BITCH.

Cole looks like he just got hit with a baseball bat. I step in front of him and up into Marian's face. She immediately averts her watery blue eyes.

This woman has no business adopting a child. She has a rap sheet as long as any hardened criminal, and she's married to Ralph. He's a piece of shit who used to be best friends with Pat. I have no doubt he's also a twisted fuck.

"Marian," I sneer. "Long time no see. Think the last time was... what? Second grade?"

Her eyes harden, and she goes to say something, but Cole steps in front of us.

"We just wanted to talk to Ralph."

I feel Cole shove me back. He knows I'm about to lose my shit.

"He's not here."

I look around Cole's shoulder. "We weren't asking."

Marian sneers, but I know she won't call the cops on us. She hates the cops. She got arrested too many times and made enemies of too many of them. Plus, now she apparently has an adoption going through, and she needs to stay off their radar.

"Jay," Cole warns.

I know what I'm doing. I know how far I can push her. I give her a dead-eyed smile and throw her a wink.

"Why don't you let us in?" Cole says.

Marian hesitates.

I shrug. "Or we can leave our car right here. Get every cop on the block eyeballing your house."

"Fuckers," Marian hisses but motions us inside. "Move that."

I do, but only because I want to scope out what other cars they have. There's a three-car garage, and I pull the car inside, parking right next to an upscale SUV. We'll take that one next.

When I step inside the house, I wander through the sprawling living room to find everyone in the kitchen. Cole is leaning stiffly against the kitchen wall, Jo standing quietly behind him. Marian stands in the kitchen with her arm wrapped around Sam.

"He's not here." Marian throws a hand in the air. "I don't know what to tell you. He's at a conference until tomorrow morning." She looks down. "Honey, can you go play your games?"

Sam hesitates.

She kisses him on the forehead. "Now, son."

The boy waits a moment before he obeys, walking stiffly past me to get to the living room. Cole watches the exchange with a strained look on his face, and it makes me murderous.

I'm going to kill his mom.

Once Sam is gone, Cole asks, "Can you call him?"

"What do you need him for?"

Cole shrugs. "Call it a keep-my-mouth-shut present."

Marian stiffens.

"So call him."

"I can't. He's preaching on live television, and he has a red-eye home immediately after. He already told me he'd be hard to contact."

Fucking hell. I'm sure that's not the reason he'll be hard to contact, but it's irrelevant. None of this is going to be fast.

I glance at Jo and see the fatigue in her eyes. Cole glances at Jo too, then at me, his gaze hard. "We'll wait."

Marian doesn't seem happy with the idea, and neither am I. But if it makes her uncomfortable, I'll indulge.

"It'll be like one big happy family," I deadpan.

Cole and Marian shoot me a glare, and in that moment, they look the same. It takes me back for a second.

"There's a guest bedroom down the hall." Marian gestures.

The guest bedroom turns out to be a mother-in-law suite.

I herd Cole and Jo inside, then slam the door.

Cole flops down onto the beige couch. The room is full of kids' toys in muted colors.

"Fuck!" Cole yanks a toy out from under him and hurls it at the wall.

Jo sucks in a breath.

I try my best at a placating voice, "Cole."

"They're adopting a kid." Cole runs his hands through his hair. He laughs bitterly, then jumps up again. "A fucking kid. Jesus Christ." He paces. "I stink. Is there a shower in here?"

I glance around. The suite is lavish and bright, with a few doors branching off. It's clear a lot of money was put into it.

"Call me when we have dinner figured out."

Cole spots the bathroom, goes inside, and slams the door.

26

Jayden is frozen, staring at the door Cole disappeared into.

I've only just met Cole's mom, but I hate her.

"Fuck." Jayden clenches his fists. "I'm going to get us something to eat." He storms to the door we came in, then turns abruptly, fixing me with a stern look. "If you try to run, I'll keep you drugged until we get to Mexico. Got it?"

I glare at him. He's being a dick for no reason. "Got it."

Fucking asshole.

Jayden looks at me for a while longer, then steps out of the room.

I hear Cole turn the shower on. The tortured look in his eyes made my chest hurt.

I swallow, then go to the door. I knock softly.

"Fuck off, Jay."

I hear a shower door roll shut, and I test the door handle. It's unlocked. Pushing the door open, I step inside.

The bathroom is just as fancy as the other room, lined with

mirrors, eggshell accents, and gilded accessories. Cole is in the shower, and the glass is fogged up.

"I said fuck off," Cole snaps.

I cross my arms.

"Fucker, did you not—" he turns and sees me. "Jo?"

I raise an eyebrow.

Cole cracks the shower door open to see me better. His face looks tortured, but he immediately tries to cover it with a smirk. "Did you want to join me?"

"No." I lean against the counter. My chest tightens from the steam in the room. I remind myself I can breathe. I'm fine. "Just checking on you."

Cole shakes some of the water from his face, then opens the door and steps out all the way. "Checking on me? You're so fucking sweet."

"What are you—"

Cole grabs at me. "Come here."

I gasp, darting away.

Cole grins. His face is manic, and my gaze darts down his gloriously naked and muscled body. My eyes lock on his left thigh, where blood drips down.

"Cole!" I gasp.

He looks down, then back up at me. "Pretty, isn't it?"

"Pretty? What..." There is a deep slash across his leg, dark blood rolling down and mixing with the water running down him.

Cole lunges at me, wrapping me in his arms. "Shower with me."

"No." I struggle, but Cole yanks me back to the shower. He drags me inside, clothes and all. "Cole!"

I gasp as he slams me against the shower wall. He stands under the spray, water raining down on his head as he blinks it out of his eyes.

Water soaks into my clothes and the bandage on my arm, and

immediately, I can't breathe. My chest locks up, and I can't suck in a breath.

"Easy, lemon drop. Breathe with me."

My chest hurts.

"Hey." Cole raises a hand to brush the hair out of my face, letting warm drops drip down my skin. "I won't let anything bad happen to you."

I pull in fast, shallow breaths. "Can't. Breathe."

"Yes, you can." Cole grips my face. "Look at me."

I do, blinking as the spray of the water hits me. Fuck, I can't breathe!

"Jo!" Cole squeezes so hard pain runs through my cheeks.

"There she is. Good girl."

I suck in a few more breaths.

Cole's expression looks pained. "I'm sorry, little one. I'm sorry." He looks me up and down. "I didn't mean...fuck."

I want to get out of the water. I need to. I struggle, and Cole winces, but he doesn't let me go.

"Here." He grabs something off the shower shelf and holds it out to me.

I blink. It's his knife.

"Cut me."

"What?" I snap my gaze to Cole's. For once, his cocky mask has slipped away. He looks tortured.

"Fucking cut me, Jo. Make me hurt for what I did."

"No!" I try to pull away, but he cages me in with his arms, the knife slamming into the shower wall with a bang.

Cole drops his head to mine, blue, pained eyes boring into mine. "Please." Then he says softer, so soft I almost don't hear it over the spray of the water, "Make it better."

I swallow.

Cole grabs my hand and puts the knife in it, wrapping my fingers around it. I stare at it.

Cole continues to stand in the spray, shielding me from most of it. I realize with a start that I've been breathing fine.

"Do it." Cole watches me, gaze still ripped open.

I clench my jaw. "I don't think I can."

"Here." Cole pushes me to my knees, grabs my hand with the knife, and pulls it close to him.

"No." I try to yank away. This is wrong. I don't want to hurt him.

Cole keeps his grip gentle but firm, guiding the knife to the skin right below his other cut.

My heart races. Fuck, I don't want to hurt him.

Cole presses our hands and the blade to his thigh, and his dick jerks.

I snap my gaze up to his, but the water pours down on my face, and I can't see. I choke for a second, unable to breathe.

"Easy, Jo. Just look at what we're doing."

With gentle firmness, Cole presses down on my hand and drags, cutting the blade into his skin. Blood wells up immediately, splattering under the spray of the water and washing down his skin.

Cole groans, a heady sound, and his dick jerks again, hardening in front of my eyes.

Cole lifts the blade, then takes his hand off mine. "Atta girl. Now do it again."

"Cole," I watch the blood streak down his body.

"Fuck, Jo." Cole buries his hands in my hair. "Help me feel good. Please."

I hate the pleading in his voice. He sounds...broken.

I raise the knife to Cole's skin again, and the groan he lets out is one of relief and need. I press it to him just enough that it dents his skin.

"Harder," Cole grits.

So I do. I press into him, the knife barely resisting as it cuts through his skin.

"Fuck, Jo! Yes. Good fucking girl." His fingers tighten to the point of pain. His dick bobs, swollen and hard.

"Again."

I do it again, this time hesitating less, and Cole's body shakes. The low growl he lets out is primal and sends the heat pulsing straight to my core.

"Now lick it up." Cole jerks my head toward his thigh. "Lick it up, nasty girl. I want to be all over you, in your mouth and hair and eyes." Cole shoves my face into the blood on his leg. "I want to be in your head, in your body, in your fucking heart. Jesus. Suck my dick with a mouthful of me."

My clit throbs, and I try to pull away from him. He doesn't let me.

"Go on. Be my nasty girl."

I feel his blood on my face. It's slippery and warm and thick. "Cole..."

"Get out of your head," Cole snarls, smashing my face into him so hard I taste the copper. "Let go for me, Jo." Then he adds in a softer tone, "Please."

It's the last please that gets me. I stick out my tongue, licking hesitantly at first, thick blood immediately filling my mouth. Cole moans loudly, jerking his hips against me. I lick harder, getting more of a reaction out of him, tasting his blood and skin. He tastes like water and copper and sweat.

It only seems to drive him more wild. Cole lets go of my hair with one hand and jerks himself furiously with the other. I drag my tongue along the cuts and feel more scabs underneath my tongue. His thigh quivers beneath me.

"More. Please," he begs.

The power goes to my head, and I moan into his skin. I lick harder, relishing Cole's reactions. He's so sensitive to every move I make. Then I smack his hand away from his dick, reaching out to grab it myself and stroke him slowly, so slowly.

"Jesus, woman." Cole bucks his hips into me. "Don't tease me."

"What?" I carefully put the knife on the shower floor and push it away from us, tracing my other hand up his stomach. Cole shifts, and the water rains down on my head.

For a second, I panic. But I suck in a breath. I'm okay. I'm in control. I can stop this if I want.

Cole waits for me. When I start stroking him again, he lets out a breath, jerking his dick into my hand. "What a good girl."

"Is this what you want?" I seal my lips over one of the cuts and suck. I pull as much of his blood into my mouth as I can, then move over to his dick and spit it onto him.

Cole shudders, his dick twitching. "God damn, nasty girl. Just like that."

I move back to his cuts, dragging in another mouthful and then spitting it all over his dick.

I close my lips around his dick and suck. I pull him deep into my throat, bobbing and licking on him with enthusiasm.

I glance up, and Cole's head is thrown back, his entire body tense. "Shit Jo, I'm gonna come."

I pull him into my mouth and relax my throat around him.

Cole comes, his dick jerking against me, his cum pouring down my throat in spurts. I take it all, sucking him down, waiting until he's done, then popping off him and licking his tip.

Cole shudders, turns the shower off, then wraps his hand around my neck, under my chin. He pulls me up, looking down into my eyes with a softness I'm not used to seeing. Cole's blue eyes search mine, then he plants a kiss on my forehead. "You look beautiful covered in my blood."

A small smile curves against my lips.

"Jesus," Cole whispers, stroking a thumb against my cheek.

I hear my name shouted from outside the bathroom, and I jump. Before I have a chance to get up, the door slams open.

"Cole! Jo ran..."

Both of us turn to see Jayden panting. He takes us in and straightens. "Oh."

"Hey," I shrug.

"What the hell happened to you?" Jayden strides up to the shower, alarm on his face.

I blink. I'm not sure what he means.

"Just messing around." Cole bends down to grab the knife from the shower floor.

"Are you okay?" Jayden grabs my face, twisting it from side to side.

Oh fuck. The blood. I lick my lips. "I'm fine."

"Where's this coming from?" Jayden frantically smooths his fingers along my face.

"It's mine," Cole says.

Jayden continues searching me, and when he can't find anything, he slowly moves his gaze to Cole.

"Cole." Anger fills his tone. "Jesus fucking Christ, enough. Give me the knife."

Cole holds it up, away from Jayden. "Fuck all the way off, Jayden."

Jayden snarls, and I struggle to get to my feet. Cole helps me up with the hand not holding the knife, and the cold air from outside rushes in around my cold clothes. I gasp.

Both men are caught in a glaring match.

"I swear to fuck, we aren't leaving this bathroom until you give me that knife."

With the water off, I can see the other scars on Cole's leg, and my heart clenches for what he's going through. I lift my gaze to him.

"Why the fuck do you care?" Cole's jaw is tight. "I'm clearly not trying to kill myself."

"Because, fuck! You're my fucking kid brother, man; you're not supposed to be doing that." Jayden swallows hard.

Cole narrows his eyes, his body stiffening. "Was I your kid

brother when I killed Pat? Hmmm? How about when I helped you kidnap Sage? Or when I hunted Jo down when she tried to leave? Stop. Trying. To. Baby. Me." Cole's seething now.

Oh shit. Oh shit, they killed Pat?

I blink, looking at the killers in front of me. My heart rate picks up, but not because I'm afraid. The exact opposite. My clit pounds. Somewhere, deep inside, I knew they killed him. I wouldn't be surprised if there were others, too.

Something stupid enters my head. I'm not sure why I offer, but I hold my hand out to Cole. "Give me the knife. I'll keep it since you two can't get along."

Both men look at me. I lift an eyebrow and hold out my hand.

Finally, Cole moves. He puts the knife in my palm, closing my fingers around the handle.

The room stills. Jayden watches me, Cole watches Jayden, and my gaze darts between them. Is this actually going to go down?

There are a few moments of tense silence. Finally, Jayden lets out a breath and runs his hand through his hair. "Fine, but don't try to cut me, Jo. I'm not into that shit, and I'll beat your ass black and blue."

Cole winks at me. "You can try it on me."

"I'm gonna kill him," Jayden mutters as he tosses me a towel and then marches out the door.

"You'll have to pick something other than a knife to do it with," Cole grumbles, then places a kiss on top of my head. "Let's get you cleaned up."

We get ready for bed in the guest bedroom. I flop down on the bed, and relief washes over me. It feels so fucking good to be in a bed after all those days on the road. Jayden follows after Cole and shuts the door with a click. They both look tired, with dark circles under their eyes. They haven't spoken a word to each other since the shower.

I'm tired, too. Tired and cold with my wet hair. Jayden put me in one of his shirts, and I feel like I'm swimming in it. It smells like him, and secretly, I love it. He also re-dressed my arm.

I haven't let go of the knife since Cole gave it to me, and Jayden rolls his eyes at me. When neither of the boys are looking, I slide the knife under my pillow.

The boys climb into bed on either side of me. At first, I think they're going to try something, but Cole just pulls me into him and pretty quickly, their breaths become even. It feels so good to not be wearing the collar. Soon, I also drift off to sleep.

· · ·

"Here, Mom." I slide the tray of food onto Mom's nightstand. Only it's not a tray. It's the lid off one of the storage bins I found in the basement because we don't have a fancy tray.

Mom groans, still half asleep.

I can't keep the excitement out of my fingers and toes, and I bounce up and down. Tonight is the night! Mom is taking me to a cooking class, and I've been excited all week. Normally, I try not to be dramatic about anything, but this week, I'm excited. I've been begging for months to go to this class, and now I feel like my chest is floating.

To show my appreciation, I researched how to make the perfect poached egg and made it for mom. I put it over a piece of toast that I browned to perfection. I also carefully sliced an avocado that had just hit the perfect ripeness.

"Mom," I prompt again when she doesn't get up.

She groans, blinking her eyes open. "What?"

"I made you breakfast." I look at the lid again and grin. I even put a few flowers I had found outside in a water glass for her.

"Oh?" Mom sits up. "For me?"

"Yes." I beam.

Mom throws me a little smile, and I feel I've made her proud for the first time in a long time. It fills my chest with a strange, fluttering feeling.

Mom reaches over and grabs the silverware. I watch anxiously as she dips her fork down into the egg. I know it's perfect 'cause I've practiced all week, but I won't know for sure until she pierces the yolk.

When she does, it runs down over her toast in a steaming puddle. Not too runny, not too cooked.

I grin.

Mom takes a bite. "It's good, honey!"

"Thanks!" I blush. "I put the water on to boil for just under four minutes. When you cook them by themselves, it goes faster." Excitement fills me. Mom is proud of me. I can't keep the words in, "Did you know that a lot of real-life chefs can't properly poach an egg? It's actually really hard to do. I tried a bunch of different ways—sorry about all the eggs I went through, but..." I trail off when Mom picks up her phone and starts scrolling.

"So...yeah."

Mom doesn't notice; she just types on her phone.

Pain races through me. The plate sits there, with one bite taken. I bite my lip.

"What was that, honey?" Mom looks at me briefly, then back at her phone.

"Nothing." I hold back the bite of tears.

She cares. She cares. She's just tired.

Mom doesn't notice me leaving the room. Pain fills my entire chest.

She cares. She loves me. She cares.

I WAKE up in a cold sweat, gasping. There's a heavy weight around my waist. I try to get up, but the weight doesn't budge. The arm drags me back into Cole's body, and his voice whispers soothingly, "Hey, Jo, hey."

I suck in deep breaths. What the fuck is wrong with me? I don't dream frequently, but the dreams about my mom seem to be coming more frequently.

"Bad dream?" Cole whispers, stroking his hand through my hair.

"Yeah," I swallow.

"What was it about?"

I squeeze my eyes shut. "Uh..."

Cole continues to play with my hair, moving his hand up to massage my scalp. He waits for my answer. "Jo?"

"It's not a big deal." I try to sit up, but Cole tightens his arm around me, pinning me to his solid chest.

His voice is low and warm, "Tell me. No one gets to make you scared, even in your dreams. So, who do I need to kill?"

I gasp. "You can't kill my mom."

Cole stiffens slightly, then relaxes his hold and plays with my hair. He doesn't push me anymore, just runs his fingers along my hairline, making me shiver. I blink and wish I had my phone. When I have nightmares, I need to fully wake up, or when I go back to sleep, I'll get dragged back in.

Desperate to take my mind off things, I ask, "What did you do while I was..." I hesitate. Will he be mad at me for mentioning when I was gone?

Cole's body is big and warm and comforting against mine. "When you were gone?"

"Yeah."

"Oh, you know. Punched some holes in the walls, threw some things around, and stalked your social media." Cole laughs, but then his voice softens. "Thought about you every second of every day."

The room goes silent, and I swallow, conflicted emotions wrestling in my chest. What he's saying is so fucked up...but it also warms my chest.

"What did you do?" Cole asks, pulling me out of my discomfort.

"What, you didn't find out?" I snort as if he hasn't bragged about sticking his nose up in every aspect of my business.

"Well, yeah." Cole chuckles and gives me a squeeze. "But I want to hear it from you. There's only so much that stalking will give you."

That stupid warmth rolls across me again. It's fucked up that I enjoy it when people care, even if their "caring" is a giant red flag.

I sigh. "I took care of this older lady, a friend of Carissa. I cleaned and cooked for her and did everything she couldn't do herself."

"Cooked?" Before I realize what he's doing, Cole rolls me around to face him, my head resting on one of his arms.

"Shhh," I hush, hearing Jayden shifting, but I still stifle a giggle.

In the dark, Cole grins at me. "Tell me what you cooked."

"I don't know," I shift. "All kinds of things. Why are you looking at me like that?"

"Jo, I'm so fucking hungry right now; if you don't tell me every single meal you cooked, I'm going to smack that ass red, then eat you until I'm full."

"Is that a promise?"

Heat flares in Cole's eyes.

I roll mine and sit up slightly. "Jayden brought snacks in–"

Cole yanks me back down, looking into my eyes. "I'm hungry for *your* food. I've missed it."

I stare at Cole. "All you've tried of mine is some shit I could throw together with Jayden's shit shopping."

Cole licks his lips. "Was delicious. I need you to make it again."

"I can do better."

Cole groans. "Don't tease me. As soon as we get settled, and I mean the *minute*, you're making me something."

I roll my eyes but feel a grin creeping at my mouth. "What's your favorite food?"

Cole grins, "You."

I smack him lightly. "You know what I mean!"

Cole laughs quietly. "Fine. Other than you..." He rolls his eyes back, then I can practically hear the hunger in his voice. "Stouffer's lasagna."

I laugh. "No way."

"Yes way!"

"That's so basic."

Cole shrugs. "Okay, Miss *Chef*. Sorry I didn't live up to your standards. What were you expecting me to say? Fucking..." he searches for a little.

I can't help but laugh again. "You don't know anything fancy, do you?"

Cole flops on his back dramatically. "I grew up on microwaved food and meals out of a can. Sue me."

My mood sobers instantly. I know his upbringing wasn't good. It was insensitive of me to joke like that.

"Oh, hey." Cole glances over at me. "That was a joke. Tell me about *your* favorite meal."

I pick at the sheet under us. "I don't know."

"C'mon, fucking tell me." Cole puts one of his hands over mine. It's silent for a bit until I glance up into his eyes. I see nothing but interest.

"Well..." I bite my lip and think. Which one is my favorite? It's so hard to pick. I love so many for so many different reasons. But I keep coming back to the simple ones. "Mac 'n cheese?"

Cole shoves my shoulder in fake outrage. "And you call me basic?"

I snort. "Not the normal kind! But that one is pretty banging, too. I make mine special."

"Tell me," Cole says. He looks so enraptured that I laugh softly. "Well, I shred my own cheese and use corkscrew noodles. Easier to get them filled with sauce."

Cole licks his lips. "Sold. What are corkscrew noodles?"

I laugh. "They're like the normal ones, but bigger."

"Is it like the baked kind?"

"Yeah! But it's not dry." I feel hunger and nostalgia dance through me just talking about it. "There's evaporated milk and cream, and I mix my own seasoning. It's crispy and creamy and stringy. It's so good." My mouth waters just thinking about it. Fuck, I want to make that again.

Cole is silent, and I look at him. He's looking at me, his eyes soft. Then, he says something that makes me freeze. "I see why everyone fell in love with you."

I blink, my mouth suddenly dry. The silence stretches on. "What?" The word comes out squeaky.

Cole suddenly reaches to my face, and I flinch back.

"Just fixing your hair, lemon drop," he says softly, brushing my hair aside. "I can see why everyone fell in love with you online. You're beautiful when you talk about the things that you love."

I swallow hard. Despite myself, warmth runs through my chest. Discomfort also battles for control. No one has ever implied something like this before, and I don't know what to do. Mom and Dad always said they loved me, but it never meant anything. My exes always said it so absently.

I swallow again, asking softly, "Why'd you come after me?"

Cole's throat bobs slowly. "Because I wanted you, Mary Jo Hall. Always have."

A rush of fear and warmth overcomes me, battling even harder for control. I don't say anything. I can't.

A bit of pain graces Cole's face, and he asks, "Why'd you hide?"

I stare at the dark ceiling, listening to Jayden's breathing. "Because I was scared."

"Of what?"

My stomach clenches, and the silence drags on. Then softly, so softly, I whisper, "This."

Cole is silent. When I finally get the courage to look at him, he's watching me intently. I see the hurt in his eyes again, and I feel another sharp bite of pain again.

"It's not you," I say quickly. "Well, I don't know. I guess..." I glance down. "I don't know how to say it."

"Try," he whispers.

I pull in a breath. I can't say it. That I'm afraid this isn't real. That I'm just a game he'll get bored of as soon as he wins.

"I'm afraid." It's all I can get out.

Cole softly grabs my hand. "I will never hurt you, Jo. Not where it counts." He reaches out and taps my chest. "Not here."

I stare at the sheets.

"Look at me," Cole demands, his tone harsh. I glance up. Cole's eyes soften. "I promise I'll never get tired of you. And if I do, you can stab me with that knife under your pillow. I'm not a liar, Jo. You're the first woman I've ever been interested in."

"Why?" My voice comes out soft.

Cole's gaze grows distant for a second, then comes back to me. "Because I see you, Jo. When I look into your eyes, *I see you.* I see a girl with fire and spunk. One who's had to fight for every scrap of love she's ever been given. One who's still funny and sassy despite all that. And when I look at you, I see a little bit of me." Cole clears his throat.

We fall into silence as I debate what to say next, if anything at all. We've gotten too vulnerable way too fast, and it scares me.

Almost as if he can read my mind, Cole squeezes my hand and then lets go. "Hey, enough of the pillow talk. Unless you want to get up and make me that heavenly mac 'n cheese, let's get back to sleep, hmmm?" Cole puts his arm around me and draws me in.

I settle into him, stiff at first but relaxing slowly. We both lay there for a while, and I think Cole has gone to sleep. I'm drifting in and out of sleep when I faintly hear, "I'll chase you to the ends of the earth, Jo. Please stop hiding from me." Then, even softer, "I need you."

28

Seven Years Old

"So, what's your favorite game?"

I glance at Pat. He's taken us fishing, and we're set up on the side of the river. He's Mom's friend, and we just met, but he's been really nice to me.

I watch my bobber. "Well, I like Tetris. But I don't really play that often."

"Oh yeah?" Pat's bobber sinks for a second, then comes back up.

"Yeah." I reel my line in and cast again.

"Why not?"

I glance at him. He's persistent. No adult has shown this much interest in me before.

"I don't have a Gameboy."

"Oh! Well, I think we can fix that."

I watch my bobber silently. Mom says that kind of thing to me all the time. I've learned she never means it.

We fish for a while longer, neither of us catching anything, but *it's peaceful. Pat talks to me about my life, school, and my friends. Then after, he takes me to the store and buys me a Gameboy. "I love you, Jayden," he chuckles as he pats me on the head.*

I barely believe it's real.

I can't believe how nice that was. For the first time in a while, my heart warms. Maybe things will be looking up from here.

JAYDEN

29

I stare at the ceiling long after Cole and Jo fall asleep. I'm covered in a cold sweat as if I ran a mile when I literally just lay here.

I heard their whole whispered conversation. The L Word was thrown around, and it made me sick. Jo trusts him. I mean, she doesn't fully, but she will. I know she will. Cole is anything, if not persistent.

It's disgusting.

I roll over, huffing out a breath. She'll never talk to me like that. I know why she doesn't. I'm not like Cole. I can't be. It's not my nature to be soft, even though I've also watched her closely. Memorized every video she made so I could repeat it line by line. I knew her favorite thing to make was mac 'n cheese. She always made videos about it between the ramen videos when she seemed down.

Fucking hell, I might be getting soft. I can't be soft. When people are soft, they get hurt.

I feel a drop of sweat roll down my forehead, and I throw the covers off me and get out of bed.

When Cole and Jo started whispering, I wanted to run. I wanted to fight. To shove my hand over Jo's mouth and shut her up. But I didn't. I froze, unable to move as I listened to them. Stuck. Frozen. Trapped. Like I have been my whole life.

My heart races as I think about it, and hot anger sparks inside me.

What the hell is wrong with me? I pace back and forth. I wanted to sleep. Need to. I haven't slept much since we picked Jo up a few days ago. I can hardly think straight.

But I need to plan. Need to nail down where we're going and how we're getting there.

Maybe a shower will help wake me up.

The shower doesn't help. My head is still just as foggy, and the only shampoo is some stupid, flowery soap that makes me smell like a walking Bath and Body Works. It clouds my head even more.

It's three AM by the time I storm out of the bathroom. I stalk to the living room, where I spotted a laptop earlier. It's password-protected. I snatch Marian's purse off the counter and find her birthday. It works on the first try.

I smirk. When I worked as a cop, I could guess people's phone passwords nine times out of ten. If it wasn't 1111, then it was some variation of their birthday, their loved one's birthday, or their social security number. Idiots.

I bring the laptop back to bed and hop on the dark web, searching for ways out of the country. It takes me a minute to figure out what to search for. I know for a fact that the feds crawl all over the dark web, hence why people talk in code. The listings themselves are difficult to trace, but the people listing their services don't want to advertise their location.

Which is fucking important when it comes to travel.

I stare at the words on the screen until they swirl in my head, and I can't see straight. I think I find a few listings and message the vendors. They all want an insane amount of Bitcoin for three passengers. It's like they can smell the desperation.

These goddamn dirty thieves.

Ralph better have the kind of money I think he does, or he and I are going to have an interesting talk with the end of my gun. My dick twitches.

Yes, I think that's exactly what I need. A little violence to wake me up out of this fog.

I wake up, and Jayden is slumped over next to us with a laptop on his lap.

I shake my head. He never turns off. I don't think he's turned off since Jo came into our lives. Honestly, I thought he would completely self-destruct until Jo.

I roll out of bed and gently pull the computer away from Jayden.

He needs to rest. He wouldn't rest even if I locked him in a room with a bed. He might sleep, but he won't rest. At least, not until after he makes his fists bloody from pounding on the door.

Jayden's eyes flutter open.

"Go back to sleep," I demand.

"What time is it?" Jayden blinks and sits up, his eyes red.

"Seven."

Jo moans and pulls the blankets up over her head. It makes me smirk. She's so cute when she's grumpy.

"I'll get breakfast. Stay in bed."

"I'm getting up." Jayden throws the blankets off.

I shake my head. I can't help him if he doesn't want to help himself.

I move to the kitchen. I'm grateful that it's quiet and everyone seems to be asleep. I don't want to see my mom. Fuck, I'm not sure I should even call her that. It's not like she ever did anything motherly for me, not like what she's doing for Sam.

My chest hurts.

I need to stop being stupid. Marian stopped being my mom years ago, probably right after she pushed me out. It's been three decades. I should be over it by now.

I get to work making a bunch of eggs. I don't know how to make them well, but I know Jo is tired of living off snacks and fast food.

I wonder when Ralph is coming back and what angle to take with him. I try to remember anything I can about him, but he's just a blurry memory from when I was a kid. I caught him staring at me a lot, but he never touched me or said anything to me—not like Pat.

That familiar, sick feeling rolls through me again, and my desire to protect Jo only increases.

But Sam... I don't know if he's doing anything, but the whole thing is odd. And that's not just because I'm jealous. Right?

I find some spices in the cabinet, smirking when I find onion powder, and throw some random seasonings into the eggs. By the time I'm finishing up, people are starting to move around.

I carry the food back to the room, and Jo is still in bed. I flop down next to her, trying not to spill the eggs.

"Wakey, wakey!"

Jo groans.

I chuckle, and some of the anxiety goes away. "I made you something."

Jo cracks a pretty blue eye open. "What is it?"

"Eggs." I hover the plate in front of her. "Scrambled."

She sits up and looks more awake. "I love scrambled eggs."

"But first," I whip out the onion powder.

Jo's eyes get big. "What?"

"Don't worry, I won't fuck you with it. This time." I wink at her. "Unless you want to hit me over the head with it."

"Give me that." Jo grabs for the plate.

I produce a fork with a flourish.

Jo takes it from me with a small smile. I watch her attentively as she takes a bite. There's a weird moment where I actually feel... afraid. Which is weird. I never feel afraid. But I want her to like it.

For a second, Jo freezes. There's a flash of...something in her eyes. "What's in this?"

"Special ingredient." I have no idea. Whatever was in the cabinet, I put in the eggs. "Is it bad?"

"It's great." Jo chuckles and gives me a smile.

I relax.

Jayden walks past the bed, a floral scent wafting by in his wake. Jo wrinkles her nose. "Are you wearing perfume?"

Come to think of it, I smelled it when I woke up, too.

"Shut up," Jayden mumbles as he stalks out of the room.

"Grumpy bastard." I swipe the fork from Jo and take a bite. As soon as I do, I nearly choke. I spit my bite out on the plate. The eggs taste bitter and herbal. They're absolutely nasty.

Jo's trying to choke back a laugh, her face growing red.

"What the fuck?" I cough.

"Special ingredient?"

"Fuck off," I snatch the plate away, slightly hurt and embarrassed.

"Hey, I liked it." Jo puts her hand on my arm.

I pull away from her, cheeks burning.

"No, I mean it." Jo scoots forward on the bed and grabs my jaw, pulling my face toward her. "You made it for me. That means everything."

I meet her gaze, ready to laugh it off, but she looks sincere. Slowly, I drop my shoulders. "If only I knew a fucking chef."

Jo's eyes twinkle.

I narrow my eyes at her. "If you're laughing at me, you're going to get punished."

Jo's eyes shine, and her mouth is tight.

The blood rushes to my dick. Oh, this hoe wants to get spanked. A slow grin moves across my face.

I move over her, making her fall back on her elbows. I drop my head to the space between her breasts and suck in a breath. "You want me to choke you and make you cry? Make your pretty little face red as you gasp for air?"

Jo's pupils dilate.

The bathroom door slams. Jo jumps slightly, and I glance over my shoulder to see Jayden stalk out of the room.

Jo clears her throat and starts to sit up.

"No you don't." I grab Jo by the throat and squeeze. Her eyes dart to mine, but she already looks more guarded.

Part of me wants to punch Jayden, and part of me wants to get Jo back to the spot she was in before. When she was happy.

Jo wiggles to sit up.

"Fuck no." I hold her down, ripping the blankets off her, and yank up Jayden's shirt.

"Cole," Jo gasps, but her pussy is already glistening for me. I dive in, eating her out, trying desperately to make her forget. Trying to make her happy again. I need her to be happy again. Jo's happiness is like crack, and I need it more than I need my next breath.

Jo comes three times before I let her up. She heaves for breath, eyes watery and cheeks flushed.

I grin at her.

She laughs weakly and sits up. "Damn."

I smirk. "Should you fight me when I tell you to do something?"

She smiles sweetly. "Absolutely."

I laugh. Fucking hell, I'm crazy about this fucking woman. I grab her chin and yank her to me, placing a harsh kiss on her lips.

When I finally let her up for air, Jo smooths her hair down and glances at the door. "So...is he going to be like this forever?"

I sigh and flop down next to her. I don't want to talk about Jayden. I don't know what his deal is.

Jo starts to pull her panties up until I shoot her a warning look. Slowly, she stops. Her obedience makes my dick even harder than it already was. I debate what I should tell her. It's not my life, but I'm afraid she'll never trust him if she doesn't know some of it.

I run my hand through my hair. "Jayden...has a hard time with trust. Always has, since Pat."

She's silent.

I pull in a breath.

"So you're saying he doesn't trust me."

"What?" I glance over at her. "I mean, not fully. He doesn't trust anyone fully. I'm sure he thinks you'll try to run again." I eye her.

Jo eyes me right back. "If I said I wouldn't, would you believe me?"

I chuckle. "No."

She grins. We're silent for a bit. Then, she asks bitterly, "What did I do to make him hate me?"

My chest clenches. She thinks he doesn't like her? After he chased her to the ends of the country, poured every bit of energy into finding her, and centered his whole routine around her?

I swallow. But she doesn't know how careless he was with Sage. How little he cared for anyone until she came around.

"Jayden is stuck in his nightmares." I reach out to touch Jo's waist, tracing my hand along the soft skin, thinking about what to say. "He relives them constantly. It's not that he doesn't like you. It's just...his brain doesn't have room for anything except survival."

Jo doesn't say anything for a long time. When I look up at her, her eyes are guarded. "Will he ever?"

"Ever what, lemon drop?"

"Have room for something other than survival?"

I swallow. I'd wondered the same thing until he met her. I thought, for a bit, that there was some hope. But now, with the way he's been acting, I'm worried.

But I won't tell her that. Instead, I say, "I think he will, with some help. But he won't accept it from me."

There's silence.

"Could it be 'cause you're a dick?" Jo looks up at me with innocent eyes.

I laugh and slam a pillow into her. She's such a fucking brat. And I love her for it.

I'm not a dick.

Well, maybe I am. But my brat loves it, and therefore, I won't be changing, ever.

AFTER COLE GIVES JO THE EGGS, I STRIDE OUT OF THE ROOM. I'm hungry, and I refuse to eat the food Cole made for Jo. She needs it. All she's been eating on this trip has been snacks. Plus, their show of affection makes me feel sick.

As I'm in the hallway about to enter the kitchen, I hear a male voice bark, "Sam!"

I spot Ralph in the kitchen. He slams the refrigerator door shut. Ralph is about my height, with slicked-back gray hair and a toned body despite his age. He looks good, which is why he still makes money schmoozing lonely housewives for their money.

"How many times do I have to tell you?" Ralph yells. "We aren't refrigerating the damn house."

Something cold skitters down my spine. The sounds of a shooter video game explode in the background.

"Maybe that damn game is too distracting," Ralph tosses something on the kitchen island.

All my muscles lock up, and a nauseating feeling rolls over me. The voice in my head screams at me to run, fight—to get away.

But I can't. I stand there, frozen, staring.

The sound of the game gets louder, the sounds of gunfire ringing in my ears.

Move, Jayden.

But it's like my body is stuck in cement, my mind wanting to run anywhere but here. Just like I was.

Just like I've been my whole life.

I shake my head violently. What in the actual fuck is wrong with me?

Weak. Fucking weak! Hatred settles in my heart. It grips its claws into me and takes over my vision.

I am not weak.

I stalk into the kitchen, rage flowing through my blood. Ralph is at the kitchen table, eating a bowl of cereal. He glances up.

"Hey, Ralph," my voice is harsh. Harsher than I mean it to be, but I can't help it. My blood is on fire. I need to keep things cool to work this situation correctly, but I can't get my body to relax.

Ralph freezes for a half second at the look on my face, then collects himself. "Oh hey, Jayden. Marian said you guys got in last night."

I pull out the chair next to him, leaning back and putting my hands behind my head to keep them from shaking. Anger heats my skin.

"You guys have a good trip?" Ralph takes another bite, using that fake soft voice preachers do, and I hate it. There's nothing soft about this snake.

"She tell you why we were here?" I let my eyelids drift halfway shut, but all I can see is jamming that spoon up his nose and scraping his brain out from the inside.

Jesus Jayden. Get control, or you'll ruin this whole thing.

Ralph tries to act relaxed, but he's stopped eating and keeps glancing at my waistband, checking for weapons. That sends a thrill through me.

So he is scared. Cute.

"Yeah," Ralph says, "said you needed a little cash."

A little? I flick him a look.

Ralph glances at the living room where Sam is playing his game. "I might be able to help you guys out. The Lord has been good to us."

I raise my eyebrow. "Does the Lord approve of your porn history there, Ralphy boy?"

Ralph goes utterly still. He doesn't even flicker an eyelash; he just stares at me with dark eyes. Then, something snaps, and he lets out a laugh. "You got me for a second, Jay." He shakes his head, continuing to laugh.

I remain deadpan. I attempted to find his porn history last night. The entire computer was squeaky clean. Which was odd. I know he's up to something. It's gotta be on his phone.

"Still got the jokes, I see." Ralph continues to laugh.

I stare at him. I've never joked a day in my life. Ralph is nervous and trying to play it cool.

Ralph pats his knee. "I can't believe it's been so many years since I've seen you! You must have been in high school."

Weak. He knew me when I was weak.

I don't respond. I want to see what his forehead would look like turned inside out. Would his skull rip cleanly from his brain, or would there be bits still attached?

I lean over, hands shaking. Instead of doing what I want to, I grab Ralph's bowl of cereal and drag it over to me. Making eye contact with Ralph, I grab the spoon and take a bite. I can't taste it; my mouth is moving on autopilot.

Ralph watches me.

"Hmm, soggy." I stand. "Let's talk about this somewhere more private, shall we?"

I don't think I can hold back any longer.

Instead of moving, Ralph leans back in his chair. "Sorry to hear about your dad."

Heat instantly races under my skin. I hate people calling him my dad. He was no dad to me. Smooth anger takes over, and focus slides into place. "Yeah, it's a shame. Anything could have happened to him." I arch a brow, looking at Ralph. He's been watching me closely.

I know he knows. He's not stupid. He knows the cops are after me.

Ralph shakes his head. "It's a shame you guys have been so distant. We didn't want to keep Sam a secret, but Cole cut Marian out, and we didn't have the right time to tell him."

I narrow my eyes. "We tried calling."

"Did you? Speaking of, why don't you get Cole? I'd like to see him again after so long." Ralph's pupils widen.

At the sight, red-hot fury runs through me. Almost like I'm watching from outside my body, I see my fist fly through the air and punch Ralph in the face. There's a satisfying snap, and Ralph crashes out of his chair, clutching his face.

Vigor fills me. I follow Ralph down, my whole body craving more. Needing more.

"Get up, Ralphy boy. Fight like a man."

Ralph groans. I stand over him, trembling. I want him to take his hands off his face and fight me. Fucking hell, maybe he'll land a punch and make it fun.

Ralph backs away, still covering his face. "What...the hell?"

Oh, don't run. I need more.

When Ralph puts his hands down to get up, I see the red trail of blood down his nose. He stands, trembling, trying to get away.

I lunge at him, and he falls backward like a coward, stumbling into a kitchen chair with a clatter.

From the living room, Sam is watching us over the couch.

I get in Ralph's face, my voice low, "Fight me, Ralph. Fight me so your boy doesn't think you're a scared little bitch."

Ralph's eyes are wide with hate and fear.

"Maybe you want it that way, though." I suck in a breath through my nose, smelling the blood. My skin is on fire. There's no way Ralph isn't just like Pat. No way he didn't adopt a boy the same age as when Cole and I got abused. "Want him to see you weak. You think maybe he'll want to fuck you more if you act like a child."

"Wait," Ralph sputters.

I punch Ralph again, the rage roaring through my blood. If he ever touched Cole, I'll rip his insides out through his asshole. A haze settles over my vision, and I raise my hand to hit him again.

Vaguely, I feel a hand on my shoulder pulling me back. I whirl and swing on the person.

Cole ducks, dodging my blow. Immediately, he slams a hand into my chest, knocking me back. "Chill, dude."

I heave for breath, and I want to lunge at him. How dare he fucking stop me?

Cole glances at Ralph and then back at me. There's a tightness around his eyes. "You didn't tell me you were going to have all the fun without me."

I bounce on my toes. That haze is easing. I don't want it to leave. I want to kill Ralph. Pound his face into the ground. Listen to him scream.

Cole glances at Sam, who's standing on the couch.

"Let's go talk, Ralph. First, tell Sam that you're okay."

Ralph wipes his nose, anger flashing across his face. "What the fuck? This guy is insane! Call the cops!"

Blind rage rips through me. He will not call the cops and get Jo taken away. Cole puts a firm hand on my chest. It feels like an anchor. An anchor I don't fucking want. It's dragging me down.

"If we're going to play, we're going to play the right way." Cole leans in closer and hisses, "Not in front of the kid, asshole."

I shake. Oh, we're going to play. And I have no intention of doing it the right way.

When Cole said he was going to get us some more food, I threw on a pair of his sweatpants and followed him. I walked in on Cole hauling Jayden off some old man. There's blood all over the man, who must be Ralph, and Jayden is seething.

I'm stuck, taking in all the blood, unsure if I should join in or run.

"Let's go." Cole shoves a bleeding Ralph in my direction. Jayden also turns, and when he locks eyes with me, his dark eyes are alive, angry, and haunted. I immediately take a step back.

"What are you looking at?" Jayden snarls.

I jump. What the hell just happened in the few minutes he's been gone?

"Go," Jayden growls.

I dart back to our room, skirting along the back of the couch.

The men follow, shoving Ralph in before them and slamming the door.

I try to blend in with the furniture.

Jayden locks eyes with me. "Where's your collar, kitten?"

What? I glance at the other two. Ralph is looking as lost as I feel. What the hell is going on?

Jayden strides up to me, and I try to dart backward, but he snatches me up by the neck. He snarls through clenched teeth, "Don't make me ask again."

"I don't know! In the car?" I try to claw Jayden's hand off my throat, but he doesn't let me go. Instead, he watches me struggle, eyes lighting up when I can't budge his grip.

"Knees," Jayden demands, then jerks me to the ground. "Or did you forget your place, slut?"

My knees hit the floor with a harsh crack.

"Cock-hungry whores belong in one place: at my feet."

Humiliation burns through me.

"Jayden," Cole says with a note of warning in his tone.

I glare up at Jayden. I hate him. I hate him and his bossy, asshole self. I snarl, "Sure, big man. Whatever makes you feel better about yourself."

Jayden leans down so fast I think we're going to knock heads. "You think I won't fuck you right here to teach you a little respect?"

No one talks to me like that, and I see red. "You'll clearly fuck me anywhere and in front of anyone just to prove a point. Well, guess what? You're a selfish asshole who only cares about himself."

Jayden's eyes flash a second before his hand is around my throat again.

"Jayden!" Cole barks. "Get the fuck over here and help me."

Jayden glares at me for a second longer before glancing at Cole, who is gripping Ralph by the back of the neck. Jayden looks back at me, giving me a long look. "Don't fucking move. You hear me? You'll stay right there."

I narrow my eyes at him.

Jayden smirks meanly, then gets up.

Ralph backs up, hands in the air, trying to escape from Cole and get out of the room.

"I don't know what the problem is. I'll give you guys anything you want," Ralph sputters.

Jayden stalks over to the bedside and grabs a laptop there. "Couch," he demands.

Cole shoves Ralph to the couch. Right in front of me.

Yeah, fuck this. I stand, but before I can walk out of the room, Jayden has thrown the laptop down and is gripping me by the hair. Immediately, I turn to fight him. I kick as hard as I can, making contact with his leg, but he doesn't even flinch.

"Let me go, motherfucker." I whirl to claw at Jayden's face, and he simply stiff-arms me away from him. He grabs a decorative bowl of flowers with a gravel base off the coffee table and throws it on the floor. Tiny rocks skitter all over the floor.

"Knees, Jo."

"Fuck you!"

"It'll hurt less if you do it yourself," Jayden warns.

I glance at the small rocks. Jayden has a strong grip on my hair, causing tears to rush to my eyes. I struggle again, and Jayden yanks on my hair so hard that I yelp. Then he shoves me to the ground.

A rock digs into my right knee, shooting pain through me. I suck in a breath and struggle to get off it, but Jayden leans into me. "No. Take your punishment for being such a fucking whore."

I hiss. The rock hurts, and it's digging into my skin. I try to put all my weight on my left knee.

"Now." Jayden glances up at Ralph, who is watching us with huge eyes. "Where were we?"

Ralph trembles.

"Oh, that's right. You were going to be a good samaritan and help your brother in need."

Jayden leans into me, forcing more pressure on my knee, and I growl. Cole throws Jayden a harsh look, and Jayden doesn't respond.

My knee throbs, but it doesn't take away from my anger. Jayden is barking orders at Ralph, who gets on the computer. I can't believe I even thought about trying to get close to this monster.

My heart pounds. Jayden leans down, whispering in my ear, "Oh, kitten. Your face is all red. Did you think you could just do anything now that you've cozied up to Cole?" He grabs a handful of my hair and yanks my head back. "Tsk, tsk. Silly girl. Silly, vulnerable kitten. You know what I love best?" He leans into my face. "Breaking girls who don't know how to stop fighting."

Hatred flashes through me. Why the hell does he have to be so horrible? I blame his harsh grip on my hair for the tears that are pricking my eyes.

I can't believe I've been so stupid. How could I have let my guard down?

"Jayden, enough." Cole's voice sounds harsh.

Jayden lets go of my hair, and I face forward, overwhelmed by a rush of anger, shame, and loneliness. Horrifyingly, I want to cry.

Oh fuck. I can't cry. I can't do that. My knee throbs, and I lean into it. The pain overwhelms the need to cry just a little.

I'll never be seen here. All I'm wanted for is something to break, and I've been weak to think there could be something else.

The rest of what Jayden does goes by in a blur. At some point, Cole comes over and asks softly if I'm okay. I just nod blankly. He frowns and gets in my face. "Jo," Cole says in a warning tone.

I can't look at him. His searching gaze scares the hell out of me. I lean into the bite of pain in my knee. It keeps me grounded.

"I'm gonna kill him," Cole mutters. He pushes me gently, lifting my knee off the rock. Suddenly, panic runs through me. I need that! Oh fuck, don't take that from me. I scramble to get it, but Cole leans into me. "You don't have to sit here, little one. Let us take care of this. Go get a glass of water. I'll be right there."

I blink, and my vision is foggy. Oh fuck. I might actually cry after all that effort not to. My face burns, and I scramble to my feet.

Jayden is hovering over Ralph, who's working on the computer, but Jayden's gaze darts to mine.

"Don't even think about it," Cole snaps.

I just need to get anywhere but here. I snatch the keys and my stuff and dart out of the room. I blindly search the house until I find the garage.

And there's our car. I fumble with the keys until I get it unlocked and sit inside, panting.

I was stupid. This will never work. I was being stupid.

Unwanted feelings overwhelm me. I've never been wanted. Not by my parents, not by Kyle, and clearly not by them.

Well, maybe by Cole, but he's a package deal with Jayden.

My hands tremble. I hate feeling things. I hate being out of control. I need it to stop. I need it to stop so I can think about what to do next.

My eyes drop to the knife I brought with me, and suddenly, all I want to do is feel the bite of the blade across my skin. To feel the relief.

This is the only thing that can help me.

I grab the blade and put the cool metal against my wrist. My hands are shaking. Not because I'm afraid of the cut, but because everything is so stopped up inside me. I just need it out. I need it *out*.

Carefully, I drag the blade along my skin. The burn of the slice runs through me, and immediately, I feel relief. It feels good. It feels like when I'd pick fights with my dad and would leave bloody. It feels like *relief*.

Why the hell haven't I done this sooner? I let my head sag back against the seat.

I just need a minute. A minute to feel nothing but the bite of the blade. Then, I'll figure out what to do next.

I CAN'T STOP.

I can't stop the rage. The anger. The blind wrath. I'm not even sure what I'm mad about anymore, but I can't stop.

Cole let Jo walk out of here before I was done with her. Instead of chasing her, I lean into Ralph's face. "Where's your porn, hmmm? Delete your history? Go onto the dark web?"

Ralph shakes. We've been watching the account that I'm having him transfer his Bitcoin into. I made him damn near empty his accounts to make sure we have enough, plus a little extra to set us up for where we're going. I want a nice little home where I can lock Jo up until her resistance fucking whithers away.

Jesus Christ, it's taking a while.

"Here, let me check on something." Cole grabs the computer.

"Where'd Jo go?" I snap.

"She's cooling down, give her a minute." Cole taps on the keyboard.

I don't want to give her a fucking minute. I don't want to give her anything! I had her where I wanted her. I saw it in her eyes, and Cole ruined it.

I broke her. I fucking broke her.

Cole already gave her a leg up by dismissing her from the room, but I'll break that down quickly. Once I ensure we have the money to spirit her away, I'll teach her to obey.

My hands shake with impatience. I whirl on Ralph. "Give me your fucking phone."

Ralph shakes as he hands it over. Rage courses through my veins. I go through it, trying to find something, anything to settle me. I can't find any porn searches. I even check Reddit, WhatsApp, and Snapchat. Nothing.

I growl in frustration, then search a folder he has labeled "Extras." Kik is in there, and I open it with glee.

Oh, this stupid motherfucker.

As I go through the messages, I find nothing but dick pic after dick pic. All adults. With nasty messages back and forth.

Ralph is sitting still, staring straight ahead. I shove the phone in his face. "What the hell is this?"

Ralph takes a second to focus on what I'm showing him and swallows.

"Well?" I grip Ralph's hair and yank his head back.

"That's...nothing."

I bark out a laugh. "Really? Cause it looks like a whole lot of dick to me."

Ralph starts shaking again. "Please...it was a mistake. Just don't tell Marian."

I toss the phone down in disgust. Ralph is boring me. Just like Sage bored me. He's frozen. Not fighting me, not running, just frozen.

I've broken him. And all it took was a punch to the face.

It should mean everything, but the victory is empty. Hollow. His submission is not what I want. I want Jo's. In fact, I need it more than my next breath.

I snap to my feet.

"Please," Ralph pleads. "She doesn't know."

What a puke. I whirl and land a punch on Ralph's face. "Where is the kiddie porn?"

"What?" Ralph wails. "What are you talking about? If you want it, I don't have it."

"I don't want your fucking filth." Rage courses through me, and I don't think before I throw another punch. "Did you touch Sam?"

"Sam?" Ralph screeches.

I go for another hit.

"Wait!" He screams. "I don't know what you're talking about! Marian wanted to adopt Sam, and I said go ahead. It...looks good, you know? A happy family. Please, I'm just running a business."

I stare at him.

Ralph sobs. "Please don't hurt me."

"Why were you friends with Pat?"

Ralph sobs harder.

I lean down by his ear and chuckle as he flinches away. "Why?"

"We fucked, okay! We fucked." Ralph cries fully now.

I freeze. That's not the answer I expected.

Cole chuckles. "Does that make us Eskimo brothers?"

I snap a nasty glare at Cole, and he throws up his hands. "We've got it." He shows me the computer screen, flipping to my wallet. The Bitcoin is showing live.

I turn on Ralph. A look of relief covers his teary face. "It worked!"

Suddenly, I have no more use for Ralph.

"You're not going to say anything, are you?" I grab a decorative pillow.

Ralph gives a giddy laugh. "Never! I'd never. This stays between us. Thank you, thank you."

"You're right, it does." I grab Ralph and shove him so his back hits the couch.

"What?" His eyes widen, but not in time.

I drop the pillow over Ralph's face and put all my weight into it, dropping my knees on Ralph's chest to push all the air out of him.

Ralph screams and panics, flailing his arms and legs. He gets a good hit in, which only pisses me off further. I lean my entire weight into him.

"Jesus, Jay," Cole mutters.

"You want to run the risk he runs to the cops?"

"Course not," Cole scoffs. "But try not to look so crazy, will you? This is just business."

I snort. Like fuck it's just business.

But part of me hates myself. I'm reacting. I never react. I think through everything. But I can't stop. I can't fucking stop.

Ralph puts up a good fight, but I'm too big. When he stops moving, I continue sitting on him for a while to ensure he never draws another breath.

"Where the hell is Jo?" I snap.

"She's taking a breather!" Cole snaps right back. "You went too hard on her, Jayden. Even I'm fed up with you."

"Too hard? I almost had her!" I curl my fingers into the pillow.

"You've never been further from having her, Jayden." Cole's voice is full of disgust, and he looks down at me. "I don't know if she'll forgive you for any of this! I'm starting to not recognize you anymore." He steps into my face. "And, in fact, you're starting to act a lot like Pat."

The words hit me straight in the gut. My world grinds to a halt.

Cole shakes his head and stalks away.

He thinks I'm acting like Pat?

I'm not. I'm not acting like him.

Suddenly, I'm more angry than I've been all morning. This anger burns through me with betrayal.

How dare he? How fucking dare he?

I jump off Ralph's body and stalk after him. "Don't fucking walk away from me."

Cole ignores me and slams the bathroom door shut.

I pause, frozen between beating down the door and chasing after Jo.

Frozen.

Again.

Fucking hell! I rip myself away and stalk to the bedroom. I saw Jo grabbing something from here before she left, and I confirm my fears.

She took the keys.

A slow grin curls up my face. Oh, she'll pay for this.

34

PEACE. SAFETY.

Pain.

I've cut two more times into my left wrist, sinking further into the escape each time. I almost don't hear the garage door open.

But I do, and when my eyes pop open, I see Jayden storming toward me.

Panic floods me, and I scramble for the lock button. I hit it right as Jayden reaches the door. He slams into the car and rattles the handle.

"Jo." Jayden's voice is slightly muffled, and he has a manic grin on his face.

My heart is still pounding.

"Jo, open the door," Jayden singsongs.

I laugh a little to myself. Fucking hell. And now he's ruined what little peace I found. I try to close my eyes again.

"Jo!" A hint of alarm fills Jayden's voice. "Fuck. Blood." Jayden aggressively yanks at the door handle.

I glance around, then realize what he means. Oh shit. My wrist. I hide my arm to my chest. "It's fine."

"Either you unlock this door," Jayden growls. "Or I'll break the window in."

Jesus Christ! Clearly I'm not going to get any rest.

I moan, "I'm fucking fine. Leave me the hell alone."

"Like fuck you're fine." Even though his voice is coming through the car door, it still sounds dangerous.

"Go away, Jayden." I close my eyes and lean my head back.

A loud sound explodes near my head. I jerk my eyes open and glare at Jayden, who's shaking his fist. He hit the window. His chest is heaving, his eyes are wild, and there's a hint of...fear.

"The cuts aren't deep, Jayden. Jesus."

"It's not that."

"What is it then?" I look away from him and stare blankly through the front windshield.

Silence. I want to sleep. I want to rest. I want peace away from people who will hurt me.

Jayden's voice startles me, "You're not allowed to cut yourself."

"Oh, you're the only one who can hurt me?"

"Exactly," he growls.

What the fuck? I laugh to myself. "Oh yeah, you think you own me."

Jayden tries the handle again so aggressively that I feel the car shake. He slams his fist on the glass, and despite myself, I jump. I feel his gaze boring into me. It makes the hair on my arms prickle. But I refuse to look at him.

"You think knowing everything about you is not owning you?" He growls. "You think arranging my whole life to fit you in is not owning you? You think I'd hunt you down to the ends of the earth if I didn't *own you*?" Jayden shakes the whole car again. "I had a whole life planned for us in the cabin." His voice gets angrier. "Before everything fucking happened."

I clench my jaw. "What kind of life, Jayden? One where you

push Cole and me out? Where the only time you show any emotion is when you're angry?"

"You haven't seen fucking anger yet."

"Please," I scoff. "That's the only thing I've seen."

Jayden is silent.

I shake my head. "Are you going to kill me?"

"What?" Jayden leans into the glass.

"Are you going to kill me?" I ask slowly.

"Never," he swears softly.

I just shake my head.

"You don't believe me."

I laugh, but it's not humorous. "You'd rather kill than feel. Of course I don't believe you."

Silence.

"Big words for someone who puts up a fight at every turn."

Anger fills me again, then helplessness. Why am I even having this conversation? "Fuck you, Jayden. I'm done. Just let me live my life in peace."

"You're not done till I fucking say you're done."

"Suck a dick."

"Not my style."

My emotions bubble over. "I fucking hate you!"

"Good. Hate I can work with." Jayden rattles the door handle. "You have five seconds to open this, or I'm breaking it."

"Go to hell."

"Fully plan on it. Four."

"Leave me alone."

"Three."

"Jayden!"

His voice gets dangerously low, "Two. Look away from the door."

"Fuck off!"

"One," he growls. "Close your eyes and face away from me."

"You can't do shit." But the way Jayden backs up and ducks down scares me. He pops back up and slams something against the back window. It shatters, glass flying everywhere. I duck instinctively.

"I warned you." Jayden reaches around, unlocks my door, and rips it open. "You always have to test me, hmmm?"

I scramble to get away, but two huge, warm hands grip me by the shoulders and yank me out of the car.

I fight, kicking and clawing.

"Now, now." Jayden yanks me to the front of the car and slams me on the hood. His strong arms hold me down. "Let me show you just how much I don't care."

I twist to get away, but Jayden has hooked one arm through my right one, cranking it up on my back until fiery hot pain shoots through my shoulder.

"Relax, and I'll let it go."

"Fuck...you," I huff. I get up on my tiptoes to escape the pressure, but Jayden just follows me.

"For once in your damn life, listen."

The pain is sharp enough that I hiss in a breath and stop. As soon as I stop moving, Jayden releases some pressure.

"There you go. That's a good girl. Was that so hard?"

I feel his other hand feeling for my other arm. The one I cut.

"Fuck off." I try to pull it away, and instantly, the wave of pain slams into my shoulder.

Fucking hell. I grit my teeth and force myself to relax. As soon as I do, Jayden eases up.

"Tsk," his warm fingers trace over the bandage on my right arm, then the wrist I cut. "This'll scar. It's gonna hurt even more when I put my tattoo over where that other man touched."

"What?" I start to jerk around so I can look at him, but Jayden presses his weight into me. "Nah, stay right there. I'm not done with you yet."

"Jayden—" but he's ripping my borrowed sweats down my legs. The cool metal of the car presses on my skin. "Fuck! Jayden."

"Do you want it to hurt, Jo?"

"What?"

"Is that why you cut yourself? Do you like the pain?" Jayden rubs his dick against my bare ass, and I clench.

"You should have said something. I can make it fucking hurt." And with that, Jayden shoves his dick into my pussy, dry.

I scream. Pain overwhelms me, making me clench down hard on him. Jayden claps a hand around my mouth and groans. "Fucking hell. You feel so fucking good crying for me."

Jayden pulls out, shoving back into me ruthlessly. It hurts like a bitch, and I fight against him. He just presses into my arm more, causing pain to shoot into my shoulder.

"Relax. Let me hurt you, Jo."

I groan into his hand.

"Shut the fuck up." Jayden slams back into me. "Take it like a good whore. I know you can take it."

Tears leak from my eyes, but it's already stopped hurting. I'm embarrassingly wet around him, and I hate myself for it. Every time he thrusts into me, it bumps my arm and causes a hit of pain, which shoots straight to my pussy. Jayden's dick brushes against my G-spot, and I jerk my hips, trying to roll my clit against the car.

"Oh, do you like that?" Jayden grips my mouth so hard it presses my cheeks into my teeth. I whimper.

"Poor little slut. Says she hates me but gets soaked for my cock. Pitiful, really."

The words make shame and pleasure shoot through me, and I clench around him.

"Nah." Jayden slows his speed. "You don't get to come. Not unless you beg."

"Jayden!" I hiss around his hand, desperation running through me. I'm so close. So fucking close.

"Didn't sound like a please to me."

Fuck, I need that pain. I fight him to get more of it, but instead of twisting my arm again, Jayden just leans on me and slows his strokes even more, taking away both the pain and the pleasure. He chuckles. "Naughty girl. You can't trick me into giving you what you want."

I feel the pleasure slipping away. I clench my jaw. I hate him. I fucking hate him.

Jayden laughs, pulling out of me. Out of the corner of my eye, I see him jerking himself off furiously. His huge hand wraps around his dick while he watches me watch him. His face is flushed, and he smirks right before he shoots his cum all over my back and ass.

"Fuck," Jayden groans. "What a good little whore."

Every part of me vibrates with shame and anger. Jayden lets go of me, taking a step back.

As I stand up, the shirt falls down, and I squirm as I feel Jayden's cum against the material.

"I'll give you thirty seconds. If you don't find Cole and get him to dress that arm, I'm going to take your ass next." Jayden pulls his pants up leisurely. "Countdown starts now, kitten. Thirty."

Fuck him. Fuck him, fuck him, fuck him.

"Twenty-nine."

I don't wait. I dart into the house, holding back tears. He's the worst person I've ever met, and I hate that I'm still vibrating with the need to come.

35

JO OBEYED FOR ONCE. SHE CURLS UP WITH COLE IN THE bedroom, and he keeps throwing me shitty looks while he holds her. Like *I'm* the problem.

I'm not the fucking problem. It's her fault for continuing to fight me.

Cole just needs a good beatdown to get that stupid idea out of his head.

But we don't have time for that. We need to get down to New Mexico to meet up with the people I paid off. We also need to avoid the cops up here. Sam saw me get violent with Ralph, and it's only a matter of time before the cops are after us. Again. We need to fucking start over.

I furiously pack some food from the kitchen into my backpack. We're going to have to drive to get picked up, and we're just too high profile to be stopping to get food.

I rifle through their pantry. All they have for water is flavored water bottles that taste like TV static, and I hate it.

Fuckers. Couldn't buy the good water?

My hands shake as I pack up.

I lost control. I lost control and made an impulsive decision. I shouldn't have attacked Ralph in the main living space. Shouldn't have attacked him at all.

No. *No*, he deserved it.

I throw some goldfish and cans of soup into my backpack.

Jo thinks I don't care. But I did it. I won. I broke Jo.

My stomach sours. What I saw in her eyes didn't look like victory. Why is none of this going the way I thought?

I snatch up the backpack, and it slams into my back from the weight of all the cans. As I stalk to the key rack by the garage door, I pass by a mirror. I glimpse something familiar and freeze.

I see Pat's eyes again. Suddenly, I hear his Santa Clause chuckle in my head. *"You're gonna be just like me, boy."* He told me that the first time I got suspended for fighting.

Fuck! What the hell is happening?

I yank the garage door open and storm through. As I step down the first step, the door handle catches on my belt loop and yanks me back. I lose my balance, falling down the edge of the steps and cracking my knee on the cement edge. I try to catch myself, but the weight of the bag shifts, and I fall on my ass onto the hard cement.

Pain lances through me.

Fucking hell! My chest gets tight, and I frantically untangle myself from my backpack.

"What the fuck!" I yell at the door handle. It just sits there, partially opened.

My knee throbs. I pull my pant leg up. There's a red rub mark with purple bruising already.

Uncontainable rage starts to boil. I want to scream, fight, or hurt something. I hold it in, and my chest gets tight until my eyes burn. Against my will, a single tear traces down my cheek.

Suddenly, all the rage, all the anger, everything races out of me in a single tear, and I'm left empty.

I put my head on my knees.

None of this was supposed to go like this. We weren't supposed to be here. We were supposed to be at the cabin. We were supposed to be living unbothered. Jo could cook whatever she wanted. She could get a dog. She could do anything she wanted—other than leave us. Why does she keep trying to leave us?

She wasn't supposed to hate me, not like this.

I sit there for a long time, thinking over everything. How I might have fucked up every single part of this.

The garage door opens, and I stiffen, instantly glaring up at whoever it is.

Cole looks down at me in surprise, then with concern. He steps down to me. "You good?"

"Fine," I bite out, instinctually defensive at him seeing the show of emotion. I stand to my feet. I want to rip Cole's eyes out so he doesn't remember he saw me like this.

Cole clenches his jaw.

Fuck. Here I go again.

Cole shakes his head in disgust. "Okay, whatever. Forget I asked." He stands.

I suck in a breath. I don't want this. I don't want my best friend to look at me like this. Why can't I get myself under control?

Cole gets up.

"Wait!" I grind my teeth together.

I'm not like Pat. I'm not.

Cole stops but doesn't glance back at me.

I pull in a breath. *Don't be vulnerable. Don't be vulnerable; you'll get hurt.*

Cole shakes his head and keeps going.

"Wait." The word feels dry in my mouth. I clear my throat.

Cole hasn't turned, but he doesn't keep walking away.

I try to get the words out, but they won't come. And that makes me angry. Why can't I even fucking speak?

Weak. I'm being weak again.

I grit my teeth. "I can't be soft, okay? Is that what you wanted to hear?" As soon as the words are out, I feel like throwing up.

Cole turns his head to look at me.

I sneer at him. "You win. I can't be what you and Jo so clearly want me to be. So there. Feel better?"

"Jayden." Cole looks angry, then pauses to take a breath.

I shake my head. This is stupid.

"It's not about winning or losing." Cole runs a hand through his hair. "What is going on? Why are you so obsessed with breaking her?"

At the thought of Jo's constant defiance, anger rolls through me. Familiar, comforting anger. "Because she won't stop fucking fighting."

Cole scoffs and shakes his head. "You can't change who she is, Jayden. She's a fighter. It's her trauma response, and she'll pick it over flight or freeze. It's who she is."

I glare at Cole. He glares right back at me.

"Why do you look so confused? The trauma responses." Cole still glares at me. "Did you not pay any attention in school?"

I snarl, "I paid attention, dumb fuck. But I was too busy fighting off the little shits trying to kick your ass." But I have no idea what he's talking about.

"Jesus, maybe *I* need to kick *your* ass. You need it." Cole throws his hands in the air. "Fight, flight, or freeze. People have set reactions to trauma and stress. You have to accept her for who she is, Jay. I like her fight. And I think you do, too, if you could get out of whatever is going on in your own stupid head."

I shake my head. Fight, flight, or freeze.

Freeze.

Fuck. My body breaks out in a cold sweat, and dread overwhelms me.

"Jay?" Cole watches me closely. I hate it.

I freeze. And it makes me weak.

Cole's voice softens. "Whatever you're going through, Jay, you can go through it with us. We're safe. Neither of us will hurt you. Although, I might kick your ass for being insufferable."

I swallow painfully. She'll hurt us. I can't give her the chance to hurt us. Not again.

Cole watches me closely. "If Jo runs, then we'll catch her again. But if you make her feel safe, we won't have to deal with that 'cause she won't run."

Anger hits me again. Does he not see how much I've been trying to keep us safe? How we've been running from the cops this whole time so I can keep us safe? I growl, "I can't keep the cops from crawling up our asses."

"No." Cole shakes his head. "Make her *heart* feel safe, Jayden."

Suddenly, my mouth is dry. So fucking dry, and dread hits me again.

I don't know how to do that. I can't be fucking soft. Love gets you nothing but pain.

I clear my throat. "We need to get rid of Ralph's body."

"See, there it is. You're changing the subject because you're so afraid you have feelings for her." Cole shakes his head. "You think you can't be soft, but you don't have to be soft to make someone feel safe. You made me feel safe even when Pat..." His voice lowers. "Even then. You were my safe space. So find whatever version of Jayden that was, and be that for Jo. She needs you."

Something tightens in my chest like a vice grip. Cole glances at me with those clear blue eyes, and I see it. The trust. The love.

My stomach twists, and I feel sick. I don't deserve that look. I couldn't make him safe. I wasn't his safe space. I was there while he was getting abused, though I didn't know it at the time.

My breathing gets heavy, and a hand falls on my arm. I jump.

"Jayden."

"Get off me." Tears fill my eyes. Fuck, this is the worst feeling ever. I need something to block it. Anything. Pure agony rips through me.

"Stop blaming yourself." Cole's voice is tight. "We were kids. There was nothing you could do."

Wrong. *Wrong!* I could have said something. Could have done something when Pat's attention locked on Cole. Punched him, hit, fought, anything. But I didn't. I should have killed him. Should have told someone what Pat was doing. Anyone at all. But I didn't. I was frozen.

All the years of feelings I've tried to contain well up in me, and I heave to catch my breath.

Don't feel. Don't fucking feel.

Suddenly, Cole wraps me in a hug. He squeezes, holding me tightly. "I love you, Jay. And I'm sorry."

I'm trying so hard to catch my breath, but a sharp pain stabs my chest. I can't breathe. I can't fucking breathe.

I need to tell him.

But I can't.

Another single tear rolls out of my eye, and I stand frozen as it slips down my cheek and drips onto Cole's shoulder.

Cole just holds me, patting my back every once in a while. Comforting me. *Me.* When I'm the one who should be comforting him.

Finally, I can't take it any longer, and I shake him off.

Cole shakes his head. "I think that was worse than a beat down."

I grit my teeth, still not able to say anything.

"Cool." Cole flashes me a smile. "I'll do it more then. In the meantime. We have a body to get rid of."

Cole and I fight over what to do with Ralph's body. It's pretty much a given that the cops will pin it on us, considering I broke the first rule: don't fucking leave witnesses. So there is no sense in messing with it. We just need to get to New Mexico as fast as possible. Eventually, though, I cave in to Cole, and we waste valuable time tossing the body in the woods outside the house. I wanted to leave Ralph on the couch, but Cole didn't want to traumatize Marian. Not that Marian deserves any of his consideration. I'd kill her too, if she wasn't the one who birthed Cole. I owe him that much.

After getting Cole and Jo into Ralph's car, I go back inside for one more thing. Marian stands, shaking, holding Sam in the middle of the living room.

It takes everything I have not to tell her what a piece of shit she is. The only reason I don't is the kid standing beside her. Instead, I glare into her watery eyes and growl, "If you do one good thing for your firstborn son, wait two days to call the cops. Two fucking days. If I find out you called sooner, I'll call the state and tell them just what kind of mother you were to Cole." I toss Ralph's phone on the couch. "And by the way, he was cheating on you with other men. Do with that what you will."

I turn to leave and hear a soft "Fuck you."

I turn, and Sam is trembling. His face is red, and his hands are bunched in fists. Marian holds him back from running at me.

The corner of my mouth kicks up. Oh, this kid will make it.

I turn and slam the door on the way out.

We drive for hours. I insist on driving the first leg. Jo wants to drive too, but like fuck am I going to let her do that. After I tell her no, she sulks in the backseat, refusing to look at me.

Cole takes over when the sun starts to set, and relief washes over me when I let him. I didn't say anything, but all the road lines were starting to blur together, and I could hardly keep my eyes open. As I climb into the backseat, Jo ignores me while digging around in my backpack. She pulls out the goldfish I packed with a small, excited smile.

I smirk to myself. I know she loves those.

Jo pops a handful in her mouth, then continues rooting. I turn to look out the window.

Fuck. I'm exhausted, but I can't sleep. Closing my eyes will make everything in my head louder, and it's already so fucking loud. I miss my phone. I wish I had something to zone out to.

A familiar, two-tone chime and electronic shooting sound come from beside me. It sounds like my childhood and summer days with Cole.

I whip my head around and see Jo starting up a GameBoy in her lap.

Not just a gameboy. A red one.

Oh fuck.

"Where did you get that?" I lean over to Jo, eyes locked on the game.

Jo pulls away from me, muttering. "What do you mean? It was in your bag."

I look closer at it as the familiar load-up image fills the screen. Oh my god. It's working.

I glance up at Cole, and he gives me a small shrug. "It was on the TV stand. Sam said he never played it. Was too old."

An odd, tight feeling fills my chest. I spent many hours on this with Cole, rotting away our summers and staying up late into the night. I thought it was gone forever.

Jo opens Tetris. I watch as she watches the blocks fall, doing nothing, losing the round.

Jo restarts, messing with the controls, looking like she doesn't know what she's doing.

She loses another round quickly.

Oh shit. Has she never played Tetris before?

Jo quickly loses another round, and I reach out. "Here, let me show you."

Jo snatches the game away from me. "Go away."

I glare at her. "You're losing."

"Thanks for pointing that out, asshole."

Her disrespect causes a shot of adrenaline to run through me. "What was that?" I lean over Jo, ready to snatch her up and put that collar on her to remind her how to behave until Cole clears his throat roughly. I snap my gaze to him, and he narrows his eyes.

I'm frozen, leaning over Jo. In that moment, I force myself to stop. Force myself to think.

Soft. I'm supposed to be soft.

Instead of snatching her up like I want to, I grit my teeth and ask, "Want to rethink those words?"

Jo mutters, "Just leave me alone."

Well, that's not how it works. She doesn't get to pick a fight and just bow out of the punishment. "I get a turn," I say. "If you can beat me in this round, I won't spank your ass red for calling me an asshole."

Jo glares at me. "Well, you're obviously going to beat me."

I resist the smirk pulling at my lips and deadpan, "That's the point."

Jo huffs but shoves the game into my lap. "Clearly, I have no choice, so may as well give me the punishment now."

My cock throbs a little. "No, I'll give you a fair chance."

We play, and I beat her. Jo puts up a little hissy fit, which only serves to make my dick harder. I love when she knows she's lost to me. I also love watching her squirm as she waits for me to punish her. It makes me wait even longer just to see her sweat.

We play round after round until Jo starts nodding off. When her head falls on my shoulder, I gently take the game from her. She jerks awake enough to pull away from me and go to rest on the side of the car.

That makes me angry. I'm way more comfortable than the side of the car. She's just being stubborn.

Suddenly, I realize that Jo didn't look angry when she moved. She just looked...tired.

That's fine. I'll wait until she's asleep, and then I'll move her to my lap. Fight me then, Jo.

Or maybe I should just keep her drugged this whole trip to keep her compliant. Then she can rest that pretty little head on me whenever she needs.

While I'm thinking, Jo passes out. I pull her over onto my lap and relish in her soft, light little body. Occasionally, the headlights from another car wash over her blonde hair, lighting it up and making it look like it's glowing.

My mind is still busy, but for some reason, it's not as loud as the normal noise that fills my head. I can't stop thinking about what Cole said in the garage.

I stroke Jo's hair, and oddly, I feel quieter than I have in days.

I HAVE THE SAME NIGHTMARE ABOUT MY MOM IGNORING ME on my birthday. Only this time, she drowns me in the pool.

I wake, gasping. As I do, I realize I'm surrounded by warm arms. I blink, trying to get my bearings. I'm lying down in my seat, and...my head is on Jayden's lap.

I startle up just as Jayden moans loudly. I don't get far as his arms band around me in a vise.

I struggle and turn to face him, my heart racing.

Jayden's head is on his shoulder, and his eyes are closed. He squeezes me tighter and moans again.

I freeze. He's sleeping.

"Fuck, Toby," he mutters. "I'll kill you."

The more I move, the harder he holds me, so slowly I force myself to relax, and as I do, Jayden's grip on me eases. I watch him in the dark. His face twitches, and the corner of his mouth turns down. He looks upset. There's so much more expression on his face when he's unguarded. So much...fear.

I swallow.

Jayden whimpers again, clutching me closer.

I glare at his shirt, trying to ignore the abs and soft skin underneath. Jayden doesn't deserve my comfort. He's the worst person I've ever known.

The dome light clicks on, and I blink, turning to shield my eyes and look at Cole.

"Oh, you're up. Sorry." He clicks it back off, and I blink again, trying to adjust. "Didn't mean to wake you."

"You didn't." Jayden still won't let me sit up. "What time is it?"

"Late. Time for you to be sleeping."

"What about you?"

"I'm good, lemon drop. Go back to sleep."

"I told you I can drive," I mutter.

Cole gasps. "And hit every curb out here?" He chuckles. "I've seen your driving record, Jo. You kinda suck."

"Excuse me? I do not!"

"Three accidents in one year? Okay, my bad." Cole laughs as I yank out of Jayden's arms. "No! Don't wake him. He needs you."

I glare at Cole, and he throws me a wink. "I'm sorry, I promise. My record wasn't any better." He mutters under his breath, "When I first learned to drive."

Oh, this fucker. I smack Cole upside the head, and he ducks. "Jo!" He shushes. "Please. He needs to sleep."

I slump back in my seat, crossing my arms. "I don't care if he needs to sleep. He can suck my dick."

Cole's eyes flash in the dark, lust apparent in his gaze. "Oh yeah? Can I watch?"

I roll my eyes. Impossible. Both of them.

We drive for a bit, and Jayden continues to sleep.

"Who's Toby?" I ask.

"Toby? I don't know." Cole continues driving, and after a minute's silence, he says, "Oh shit. I guess there was a Toby in high school. He used to bully me. He was one of the first kids Jayden got sent to detention for fighting."

I scoff. Jayden fighting in high school makes so much sense.

"As if you didn't go to detention for fighting a chick, too." Cole glances at me in the mirror.

I did. She always looked down on me. So after I bloodied her nose, I told her to look down on me from the ground.

I was particularly bored that day. How the hell did he know that, though?

"Do you know everything?" I mutter.

"Thought we went over this. Yes. But Carissa also ran her trap a lot on social media."

I shake my head. Of course she did.

"She posted a picture of you guys after, at some pond. Had a nasty shiner. Girl got you good." Cole laughs.

I think back. I remember that day. We went to a summer party together. That black eye wasn't from the fight, though. I shake my head. "Nah, that girl couldn't land a punch even if she tried."

The car gets silent.

"She didn't give that to you?"

I laugh. "No, that was my dad."

Heavy silence.

Immediately, I freeze. The energy in the car shifts.

Oh shit, I shouldn't have said that.

"YOUR DAD, HUH?" COLE'S VOICE IS TIGHT.

I woke up in time to hear Jo say her dad gave her a black eye. Instantly, I'm on alert.

"It's not like that," Jo rushes to say. "It was my fault. I picked fights with him on purpose."

Cole is silent. The rage that's bubbling in my chest is unreal.

No one gets to hurt my girl. No one but me.

My words come out low, "I'll kill him."

Jo jumps and looks at me. "No! You can't kill my dad."

Yes I can.

"Why didn't you say something before?" I can hear Cole trying to keep it together.

"Because it doesn't mean anything? I wanted to fight him. Please, it's not that big of a deal," Jo pleads.

Cole scoffs as if he doesn't believe her. "You were fucking twelve."

"So?"

Twelve. She was a damn kid.

I clench my jaw and force my gaze away from her. The

shadows on her face make it look like she has a black eye now, and I can just picture it when she was a kid. If I look at her any longer, I'll get Cole to make a stop at her parents' house.

It would be a long detour. Maybe we'll have time...

Jo continues to plead with Cole. She's defensive, and that makes me angrier. Her piece of shit dad doesn't deserve that kind of defense. I'm jealous of any energy she's giving to anyone else. She's mine. Ours.

She doesn't get to defend anyone else.

I try, but I can't keep my eyes off her. Jo has stopped arguing, and now she has her arms crossed. She looks so small and helpless.

I know a lot of things about Jo, but I didn't know she fought her dad. But I can see it. Not sure why I didn't guess this about her earlier.

Jo sees me watching her and rolls her eyes. It's brief, but it makes all the blood go straight to my dick.

I snatch her up, and before she can put up too much of a fight, I lay her over my lap. "Still have a spanking you owe me."

"Get off me!" Jo struggles. It makes me hard as fuck to have her at my mercy.

I chuckle. Jo has put her one pair of shorts back on, but that won't stop this from stinging.

"Tell me why you fought your dad."

"Get off me!" Jo tries, but she can't get out from under my arm. I barely feel her attempts. I know if I checked her panties, she'd be wet.

"Guess you want the spanking now." I raise my hand.

Jo stiffens.

I wait.

"I was bored," she gasps. "I was bored, okay!"

I stare at her, suddenly even more interested. She was bored? Sounds like something I would say.

"Let me up."

"You were bored?"

"Yes! I answered the question, let me up."

I frown. She did, but I didn't say I wouldn't give it to her, and I still owe her a spanking. I slap my hand down on Jo's ass with a delicious sound.

Jo squeals, and I let her up. She scoots back, crossing her arms again. "Caveman."

"Who picks fights because they're bored?" I raise an eyebrow at her.

"I don't know! I did." There's no deceit in her tone, just embarrassment and...arousal.

"Did you win any of them?"

Jo glares at me. "Depends what you mean by win."

I pause again. I fought throughout high school. I won every time, but I never felt like I was winning. It was always a fix until my next fight, and I'd leave that one even more empty. The only time I didn't feel empty after a fight was with Jo.

She was the first time I didn't win.

I blink and cock my head. I stare at her. Really look at her.

Jo narrows her eyes. That fight I've been obsessed with for so long is burning bright in her eyes. But for the first time, when I look at her, I also see the pain. And then I realize something with horrifying clarity.

I've been trying to break something that was already broken.

Something just like me.

THE REST OF OUR TRIP IS A BLUR. JAYDEN IS EVEN MORE withdrawn than usual, but we're all exhausted. Despite my misgivings, the people Jayden found to mule us across the border were fine. We flew on an undeclared plane, landed in a field, and they gave us some money and took off again.

The first thing we did was walk to a town, where we paid for a ride to one of the big cities. It is easier to disappear in the masses.

We pay for a cheap hotel, and even though we get in around noon, all of us are beat. There are two small beds, and I throw my shit on the one farthest from the door. I know Jayden will want the one right by the door. Easier to shoot someone from, blah blah blah. The beds are small, and it's going to be a challenge to fit two people on one. Even so, they look like heaven after nothing but a car and an airplane for the past two days.

Honestly, I just need to wash my face and sleep—in that order. When I'm done with my face, I see Jo standing between the beds, clearly trying to decide which one she wants.

My first instinct is to snatch her up and yank her into my bed.

My chest hasn't stopped hurting about the fact my mom replaced me with another kid, and I want something, anything to help.

But I don't. I drop into bed, my body aching. I could easily over-power Jo and force her into bed with me. But I realize with a tight-ness in my throat that I want her to want me.

I want Jo to *actually* want me.

No gimmicks, no force, no overpowering. I want her to want me for me.

Jo still hasn't picked a bed.

I close my eyes, trying to fight off the pain. Then, there's a rustle of the sheets, and Jo climbs in behind me. A rush of relief fills me, and it's so overwhelming that I want to cry. I turn to grab her and curl my body around her. Burying my nose in her hair, tears sting my eyes.

Jo got in bed with me, and I didn't have to force her.

Some part of me dances. This can't be real. It's not real, right?

I pass out with Jo in my arms.

I'm not sure when I wake again, but it's to a deep shout. I startle up in bed, throwing myself between Jo and where the sound came from.

I'm disoriented, but nothing seems off when I blink into focus. Then Jayden shouts again. It's a fearful: *no.*

Jo scrambles up beside me. "What's going on?"

Jayden thrashes on the bed.

I drag my hand down my face. "He's dreaming again."

Jo throws the covers off, moving to get out of bed, and I grab her wrist. "What are you doing?"

Jo tries to shake me off. "It'll be fine."

She's going to get in bed with him. Fuck. I've seen how Jayden acts when he's having a nightmare. He's unpredictable.

"Cole!" Jo throws me a look that is full of frustration and help-lessness. Instantly, I let her go. Fuck, I hate that look. I hope she never gives it to me again.

Jo pads over and sits on the edge of the bed. She grabs one of Jayden's hands and holds it. I stand stiffly, watching him. But he doesn't do anything. If anything, some of the tension goes out of his body.

Jo traces patterns on the tattoos on Jayden's arms. Then she slides in next to him, and lies down.

"Jo," I growl. I'm all for her being there, but now she's just being reckless.

"It'll be fine." Jo throws me a glare. "I'm a big girl."

Oh, she thinks she is, but Jayden is twice her size. He could easily hurt her before he realizes what he's doing.

"Scoot over." I shove at Jo.

"What?" She looks over Jayden's body. "There's not enough room."

"Then you're going to get squished." I shove at Jo until there's a sliver of space on the bed. No way am I going to let her lay there alone. Jo huffs when I squeeze in beside her. Half of me is hanging off the bed, but I don't care.

Whether she likes it or not, she chose me, and now I will keep her safe. I will protect her from anything that wants to hurt her, and I will never let her choose anything other than us ever again.

We've been in our new apartment for a week. My period also started the first day we got here, and I felt murderous and refused to get out of bed. Since then, I've done nothing but eat and sleep. Cole brought me a phone to try and coax me out of bed, but I couldn't.

It's all too much. Too much change. Too much newness. Too much...everything. Not even the food is the same here. Although, every day since we've been here, my favorite snacks have been turning up at my bedside. They're the only things I'll eat.

Every time Cole checks on me, I see the torment in his gaze, although he tries to hide it. I want to fight with him about it. To tell him he caused this. Make him give me anything other than a pitying look, but he doesn't get roped in. Which throws me off even more. I'm used to them fighting me. Tormenting me. But they've done none of that. Well, Cole doesn't. I know I could get Jayden to fight me, but I almost never see him. Cole says he's out looking for jobs.

I almost miss the toxicity. I just want something to make me feel normal again.

On the evening of the seventh day, Cole drags me out of bed. He says nothing, just grabs me under the arms and legs, and heaves me up bridal style.

I squeal, "Put me down!"

"No can do, lemon drop." Cole doesn't lose his grip on me as I fight. He just carries me to the kitchen and puts me down. I glance around. I've seen the kitchen briefly from the hallway. It's an open-style kitchen with a huge island in the middle and a large window lining one of the long countertops. Golden light filters in, and I see neighboring buildings and trees. Despite myself, I admire it for a second.

"You're gonna teach me how to cook mac 'n cheese," Cole says, caging me in.

Immediately, I cross my arms. "No."

Cole laughs. "You're cute. That wasn't a request."

Despite my fatigue, I glare at him. He thinks he can order me around? After everything?

Cole smirks. "You're adorable when you think you're in charge."

This asshole. I flip him off and start to walk around the island and back to the bedroom.

"Fuck no." Cole snatches me up and hauls me back. He pins me to the island with his body, leaning up behind my ear and pulling in a breath. "Fuck, you smell so sweet, lemon drop."

"Let me go." I struggle.

"What, so you can hide again? No. Your days of hiding are over, Jo." His voice gets tight. "Now teach me how to make this damn food."

Fucking hell, trying to push against him is like trying to wrestle a wall. He won't budge.

I let out a breath and glare at the island. There's food there, with corkscrew noodles and milk and cheese. So much cheese, actually. An absurd amount.

"I tried to remember what you told me, but you didn't say what kind of cheese, so I bought them all."

I look through the ingredients. "You didn't get any spices."

I feel Cole shrug. "So we'll get some."

The fatigue hits me again. "I don't feel like going out."

"Well, lucky for you, the store is right under us."

"What?" I turn to look at Cole, and he lets me. His eyes twinkle. "Isn't that what you wanted? A grocery store close? I'm sorry it's not open 24/7, but we're not rich enough for that yet. Soon, though. Very soon."

I just blink. He fucking remembered that?

"So, spices, what kind?"

I blink a few more times, then turn back to the table. I can't believe he paid attention. He stands right behind me like an eager kid.

I frown. I don't feel like cooking, but Cole never takes no for an answer. Maybe this will get him off my ass. I give Cole a list of things to get, thinking he'll let me stay here.

But the fucker drags me downstairs with him, forcing some shoes on my feet. I'm pissed and fight him until I see the small store. I've never been to Mexico, and as I look at all the food, I can't help but get excited. There are so many things I've wanted to try from here.

Cole sees me eyeing the candy and buys every option they have. I roll my eyes when he also buys a jar of onion powder and gives me a wink. Then, Cole grabs what ingredients we can find and carries them all himself.

By the time we get the food upstairs, I'm shoving Cole's awkward ass out of the way. It's clear he doesn't know his way around the kitchen. Despite that, Cole hovers around me, asking questions and getting in my way. To get him to stop stepping on my feet, I sit him down to shred cheese, and he does so enthusiastically.

I get to work prepping the other parts of the sauce while

walking Cole through the steps. He's terrible in the kitchen, but he does everything with such energy I can't help but catch a little of his pep.

"You should put me in your cooking videos." Cole grins after pouring the water out of the noodles and dropping a third of them down the sink. "I'm kind of a pro."

Instantly, I sober. That's not a part of me anymore. It can't be since we're on the run. I've been thinking about that all week. I can't be who I used to be at all. Can't show my face. Can't teach people to cook. Can't...anything. I don't even know what I like to do in a foreign place...besides cooking.

Cole flexes his arm as he holds the pot. "I mean, look. These arms look so good carrying things around."

I shake my head, and Cole notices my mood change. "Uh oh. You afraid the other girls will be jealous?"

I scoff, snatching the pot from him. "I can't make those videos anymore."

"Why not? You love them." Cole watches me.

"You know how fast the cops would be at our door?"

Cole shrugs. "Cause of your face? Wear a mask."

I start to argue, then pause. I didn't think about that.

"I'll wear one too. It'll be hot. We can even get Jayden in on it."

My stomach is in knots. I don't want to start from scratch all over again. The idea of building followers from the ground up just makes me tired. I mutter, "Jayden would never agree to that."

"He won't have a choice." Cole grins.

I roll my eyes. "What are you gonna do? Wrestle him to the counter?"

Cole laughs. "Maybe. Why? Would you like that?"

Despite myself, the thought of them fighting with their sweaty bodies thudding together makes my cheeks flame.

"Oh, you would." Cole leans across the counter to get closer to me.

"Fuck off. Where's Jayden anyway?" I busy myself mixing the mac n' cheese with a long-handled ladle.

"Says he's looking for a job." Cole snatches the ladle from me and licks the cheese sauce off it. "But most likely hiding from you."

"Hiding?" I whirl.

Cole catches me and plants a kiss on my forehead. "You know, you look so sexy in the kitchen. I could just eat you up."

I pull away from him. "Why in the hell is Jayden hiding from me?"

Cole rolls his eyes. "Who knows. You know Jayden is afraid of feelings. And your 'feelings' for him."

I stare at Cole.

"I mean, you've always had feelings for him, but he's refused to admit that until now."

I continue to stare.

"Plusss," Cole snatches a noodle and eats it, "he also might be shopping for your birthday."

I stiffen. Oh fuck. I ask cautiously, "What is today?"

"September fourth." Cole grins.

The day before my birthday. I swallow hard. My recurring nightmare comes rolling back in. The last birthday I hoped would be a good one was the one when my mom couldn't give two shits less.

"Birthdays are stupid. Don't get me anything." I throw the food into the oven and slam the door.

"Oh, hey." Cole grabs my elbow.

I shut everything down. All the happiness I started to feel again disappears. Fuck, I had started to feel like there was something here. Cole will stop caring as soon as he gets bored.

"Whoa, where'd you go?" Cole turns me to face him.

I stare at him blankly.

Anger flashes in Cole's eyes before he dips down to kiss me. Hard. His lips cover mine, and he licks at the seam until I automatically open for him. His hand snakes down my front and palms my pussy. His magnetic energy makes heat flood my body.

I try to fight it, but that only pisses Cole off more. He pinches my clit and bites my lip, causing me to gasp.

Cole kisses me deeper, harder, and more aggressively until he's bruising my lips. It sparks feelings in me for the first time since we got here.

"Come here." Cole lifts me up, and I squeal. He drops me on the counter in front of the big window and then rips my shirt off.

"Cole," I gasp. It's dark enough outside that everything is visible with the lights on in here.

"Yeah?" He pins my hands in my lap as I struggle to get away.

I hiss, "Someone will see."

"Kinda the point, Jo." Cole yanks my shorts down, then rips my panties away.

"Cole!" I fight to get away.

Cole yanks his dick out and lines it up against my legs. "You may be embarrassed, but I have no issues showing off my woman for the world to see."

"Cole, stop." Heat creeps up the back of my neck, but the shame mixes with something else. Something more electric.

"Saying no never worked before, and it won't work now." Cole lets my hands go to lift me up and slam his dick into me.

"Fuck!" I grip Cole's shoulders, the shock of him filling me racing through my body. He lets me adjust for a second, gripping my ass and keeping me firmly connected to him.

"You ready, my little chef?"

I dig my nails into his back, and he groans. "Fuck yes, Jo. Just like that." Cole starts pumping into me. I expect him to go roughly, but he doesn't. He strokes slowly in and out again, making sure I have time to feel every pass. His nails dig little bites of pain into my ass.

"God, you feel so good," Cole moans.

"Faster," I groan.

"No. You can take it slow." Cole peppers kisses up and down my neck.

"Cole," I groan and buck my hips into him to get him to fuck me harder. It's too slow. Too sweet. Too nice.

"Yes?" There's a chuckle in his voice.

"Fuck me," I hiss.

"Hmmm. Why, when I can torture you so wonderfully right here?"

"Fucking sadist." I buck my hips into him again, and he groans. "You make it so hard to torture you." Cole grips my ass tighter and holds me in place. "Look at me."

I squeeze my eyes shut.

Cole pinches the skin of my ass so hard I gasp and open my eyes.

"There you are. I have something to say, and then we can get back to what we do best."

I stare at him.

Cole clears his throat. "I know trust is hard for you. And you have every reason not to trust me. But." He pinches again.

"Ow!"

He grins. "I'm here for the long run."

I stare at him. I don't know how to process that information. Despite myself, there's a flicker of hope.

"And." Cole has stopped moving altogether. "I know you push me away because you're scared, but I have...You're the first woman I've allowed into my life since my mom."

I freeze and glance back at him.

Cole looks at me earnestly. "I'm trying to understand, Jo. I am. But when you push me away, it makes me a little murderous, and I want to come down on you two times harder. Which," he pounds once into me, "is great when we're fucking. Not so great any other time."

I don't know what to say, but Cole doesn't act like he needs any response. He reaches down to play with my clit while he pounds into me, this time not holding back. He slams into me over and over, and the pain, mixed with the pleasure, immediately makes heat rush through my body.

Cole leans into me. "Don't look now. Our neighbors are watching."

"What?" I try to look back, but Cole grabs my chin and yanks me back to him. His voice gets angry, "My eyes only when we're fucking Jo. Don't you fucking dare give anyone else that sexy look. That belongs to me and Jayden."

As he says that, I see movement in the hallway. I freeze for a second before I recognize Jayden standing in the shadows. He leans there, watching us.

Pure heat rolls through me, and I can't tell if it's anger or fear. I'm still mad at him. For everything. For kidnapping me. For not giving me a voice. For being an ass. But among the anger is also arousal. I can't help but look at his handsome face and muscled body.

Cole chuckles into my neck. "Just noticed him?"

I shiver.

"Make him jealous, baby." Cole slams into me, and I moan, scratching my fingers along Cole's back. Jayden's dark eyes watch my every move, but he doesn't make an effort to get any closer.

Despite the fact that Cole is fucking me harder, I still sense he's being gentle with me. And I hate that. I don't need him to be fucking gentle.

I trace my lips up Cole's neck, and he groans, shivering while he fills me. I move up to his ear, where I feel his earring against my lips.

"Cole?" I whisper in his ear.

"Yeah?" He moans.

"Stop being fucking gentle." I grab his earring between my teeth and rip.

"Fuck!" Cole immediately yanks his head away. He stands there in shock for a second, then bears down and bites my throat. He bites so hard I bow my head back and yelp.

Cole chuckles, then picks me up and moves me to the island. He slams me down on it, making the breath burst out of my lungs. There's blood trickling from his piercing. "You want to get treated like a little whore, is that it?"

A forbidden thrill runs through me at the sight of Cole's blood. I'm in for it now.

I scramble back, but all niceness is gone from Cole's eyes. "Hold her down, Jayden."

Before I realize he's close, Jayden's on top of me, pinning my shoulders to the island.

"No," I say, but Jayden completely ignores me.

Cole comes back into view, holding the spoon we were using to mix the food. "Think this'll fit, Jay?"

Cole grins as my eyes widen.

"Depends which hole."

"No! Get that away from me." I try to kick Cole, but he simply hops on the island and yanks my shorts the rest of the way off. He gets between my legs and holds up the spoon dramatically. "Hmmm."

I struggle, but Jayden has my upper body pinned entirely.

"You're lucky, I'll do the small end. But only 'cause the spoon is dirty and can't have you getting an infection." Cole turns the ladle over. "But this is too small for your pussy."

"Cole, no." Fear fills me. There's no way I want the handle going anywhere near me.

Cole watches my reaction, his pupils getting bigger. "By all means, fight me, Jo. It'll only make it more fun for us." He glances behind me. "Jayden's about to blow a load in his pants."

Jayden growls, "Eyes to yourself."

Cole slaps a mocking hand over his eyes while he brings the handle up to his mouth. He licks up it, getting it wet, and pops it in his mouth.

Fuck, fuck, fuck. He plans to fuck me with that.

Cole lowers the ladle to bump into my thigh, all while covering his eyes.

I stiffen. "Cole."

He drags the ladle down to my pussy. I arch my hips. Maybe I can get him to slide it into my pussy instead of where I think he plans to put it.

Cole peeks out between his fingers, then goes back to dramatically covering his eyes.

"Stop being an idiot," Jayden growls.

Cole throws me a wink under his hand, then takes his hand away and slides the handle down to my ass.

I pucker immediately. The handle isn't huge, but it's partially flat and oval-shaped.

"Cole, please."

"Relax, Jo, and this won't hurt as badly."

Jayden leans down in my ear. "Are you begging, kitten?"

I try to thrash back and forth. Cole pauses, just brushing against my hole.

"You gonna beg me to stop, Jo?"

I stare at the handle. Cole is so hard his dick is throbbing.

"Will it help?" I grit my teeth.

"Hmmm." He raises an eyebrow and smiles. "Why don't you try it and see?"

I glare at him.

Cole pushes the handle roughly past the ring of muscle in my ass. I gasp, pain racing through me. My back arches off the island until Cole's other hand grabs my waist and pushes me back down.

Jayden groans behind me, and Cole's pupils are completely blown out. "What a fucking gorgeous sight."

Cole pushes the handle deeper, and I scream.

"Jesus," Jayden grunts.

"What a good girl. You're doing so fucking well." Cole lines his dick up with my pussy. "Be a good girl for me and take my dick too."

Cole presses into me slowly. I gasp, trying to take him as well. Once Cole's seated, he sits there, letting me adjust. I have so many sensations all at once, and it's overwhelming. The pain is overwhelming, but also the pleasure.

"You're doing so good," Cole moans. I feel his dick throb in me. "Fuck, you feel so good. So tight."

Cole moves slowly, and as he does, pleasure builds. Cole groans, pulling out and pressing back in. I gasp. The movement also causes the ladle to move, shooting electricity through me.

"Oh god, Jo. I can't wait to fill you so full of my cum it spills out of you." Cole groans, his arms shaking. He reaches one hand around to play with my clit again. "One of these days, we're going to lock you up in your room and breed you until you're full with our baby. I'll tie you to the bed so you have no choice but to accept load after load. Then you'll be stuck with us forever. No more running, even if you wanted to. We'll provide everything for you. All you'll have to be is our sexy little momma."

Cole flicks his fingers over my clit, and a thrill runs through me. His words are dirty. I don't want a baby now. I don't want to repeat history and be my mom to my kid. But still. Something about his possessive energy makes me flush with pleasure.

Cole continues playing with my clit. That and the extra sensations from my ass are enough to have me exploding all over Cole's dick.

Cole follows shortly after, coming inside me with a groan.

"Fucking hell, Jo." He pants. "Jesus."

As the pulses from my orgasm fade, Cole pulls out of me, then gently pulls on the ladle. I tense, but he pulls it out.

Cole hops down off the counter. "Carry her to the room, Jay, and we'll get her cleaned up. Someone needs their beauty sleep before we celebrate."

JAYDEN

41

I'VE BEEN HIDING FROM JO ALL WEEK. I'VE KNOWN HER FOR months and seen her at her highest highs and lowest lows. But suddenly, she's become the scariest person I know. I'd rather face a man with a gun than her.

I can't get over how she comforted me while I was dreaming in the hotel. I woke up mid-nightmare to find her curled up into me. The absolute, blinding fear I felt when I worried I had done something to hurt her while asleep scares me still. Makes me sweat.

Instead of facing her, I bring her her favorite foods every night after she's gone to bed. I try to sleep on my own, but I can't. The noise in my head is too loud. So, every night, I find myself crawling back into her bed. I leave before she wakes and go out to find a job. Or at least, that's what I tell myself. I'm mostly just avoiding her.

Nevertheless, it's some of the best sleep I've gotten since we had her at the cabin.

Cole knows. I know he knows, but he hasn't said anything to me about it. When I watched him fuck her against the window, I was equally scared and turned on. And when he called me over, I was afraid he'd call me out on my shit, and she'd see how scared I've been.

Scared. Frozen.

I researched what Cole said. I still think I'm weak, but since then, I've felt...weird. There are some moments when my head is quiet. Usually, it happens when I'm cuddled up with Jo. But now, I don't even have to be fucking her to feel it. Just around her.

Today is her birthday. I have her gift, and as I stand in my room with it, my hands sweat again.

This is so dumb. She's going to think it's stupid. I put her gift on my bed and sit down so my hands stop shaking.

What the actual fuck. I've killed people with less of a reaction than this. I debated for a while on what to wear. Cole said we had a dinner planned. At home, of course. It's already a risk that I'll be recognized going out, but I don't want to put Jo at risk, either. Not while our case is so hot. It'll be safer when it blows over.

I'm not sure what Cole got Jo. He did say there was a part that I'd have to participate in. He asked if I wanted to know what it was, and I said no. It made me sick to my stomach, but I know if I knew, I'd back out. I almost said no, as it was. Almost. But I'm trying.

I smooth back my hair for the twentieth time.

Stupid. I'm being stupid. It's just a dinner.

Fuck, I'd rather kill someone.

I snatch the gift from my dresser and march down the hall. Jo and Cole are already there. Jo's laughing while trying to teach Cole how to make something in the kitchen, and he's fucking it up, as usual. I never let Cole cook in the cabin for this very reason.

I stare at Jo, suddenly frozen to the spot. She's in a light blue dress with a cream bow in her hair. She's so beautiful. So damn beautiful.

Jo throws me a look, and the smile falters on her face. She swallows. "Oh, hey."

Suddenly, I think the button-down and slacks I wore are ridiculous. I look dumb, and they look so good. I turn on my heel to go change, but Cole says, "Hey, don't go. Help her with the table while I get her gift."

"I told you not to get me..." Jo argues, but Cole has already moved to the front door, leaving Jo and I standing awkwardly.

She bites her lip and turns back to the stove, where she's stirring something.

I'm stuck again.

I hate this. Why the fuck am I frozen? I'm in my own fucking apartment. This shouldn't be traumatic for me.

"You just gonna stand there like a creep?"

Instantly, my eyes snap to her. Jo continues to stir the pot. She throws a tiny glance over her shoulder, and from the slight twinkle in her eye, I see she's being a smart-ass.

Immediately, I stalk up behind her and fist my hand in the back of her hair, yanking her head back to look at me. When her baby blues fly up to mine, I smirk. "Wanna keep up that attitude, slut?"

Jo narrows her eyes but doesn't say anything. I laugh tightly and let her go. Smart girl. Fuck dinner, I'll throw her on this table right now and punish her until she can't remember her own damn name.

A timer goes off, and Jo opens the oven. Instantly, a wave of heat rolls over us, and I push Jo back.

She flashes me an annoyed look, but I pay her no mind. I grab the oven mitts off the counter and pull out the casserole dish. Looks like lasagna.

My mouth waters.

"I can do that myself," Jo protests as I carry it to the table.

I know she can take it out herself, but I enjoy flustering her. I enjoy taking care of her and seeing her get mad about it.

There's an odd scrambling noise at the door. We both glance up to see Cole peeking through while keeping the door cracked. "Jo! You ready for your present?"

Oh lord. What the fuck did he get her?

Jo glances at me briefly. I shrug. He didn't tell me what it was.

"I guess?"

Cole opens the door, and something darts across the living room into the kitchen. I stiffen to protect her before I realize what it is.

Jo gasps.

Jesus Christ. I run a hand down my face. It's a dog.

The golden retriever runs straight to me, jumping all over me, panting and wagging its tail. Then it shoots over to Jo, licking her hand, then sniffing around the room.

"It's a...you got me a dog?" Jo looks up as Cole moves to her, snatching her in his arms and giving her a huge kiss. "Yep! Jayden said we had to wait till we had a place to live. Now we do. Do you like him?"

"It's a him?" Jo struggles to get out of Cole's arms so she can greet the dog again. It licks all over her face as she crouches down and she laughs.

A shock of jealousy runs through me. Of course he got her a dog. She loves it. Cole's out here being perfect all the time. How in the fuck am I supposed to keep up? I can't.

I shake my head and go to step away, but the dog breaks away from Jo and runs up to me, jumping up on my legs and smiling up at me. Then, before I can react, it lifts its leg and starts peeing on my shoe.

"Jesus!" I jump back.

The dog jumps around, acting like it didn't just piss on me.

"He just marked you as his!" Cole starts belly laughing.

I glare at him. "This isn't funny."

Jo is trying not to laugh. I shoot her a glare, too. She grabs some paper towels, and I snatch them from her. I take off my shoes and clean up the mess. The dog licks my face while I'm down on the ground.

"Do you like him?" Cole asks again.

Jo's smiling deeply now. "I've always wanted a dog."

"I know." Cole beams proudly.

Jo grins and smashes a kiss to Cole's face.

That's it. I can't take it any longer. I grab my gift and try to escape barefoot, but the dog makes it hard.

"Where are you going?" Cole asks. "We just made dinner."

"I made dinner. You got in the way." Jo pulls away from him and looks at me. "Is that for me?"

My cheeks burn. I don't want to give this to her. There's no way it can compare to a fucking dog.

"Uh, yeah. But it's nothing. It's not the real gift."

Behind Jo's head, Cole arches an eyebrow.

"Okay..." Jo stands there awkwardly as I continue to hold her gift hostage. Fuck. I don't want to. I snap out of it and practically throw it at her.

I need to do anything other than watch her, so I start serving the food. As the wrapping paper falls away, there's silence.

My face burns even more. "It's stupid. Just something dumb."

Jo turns the plastic container over in her hand. "It's...flowers?"

"Like I said, dumb." I burn myself on a piece of melted cheese and hiss.

"No, these are..." I hear the plastic pop open, and she goes through all the layers. "Oh shit, these are edible?"

I don't think my face can get any more red. "Uh, yeah." I spent days researching the edible flowers that chefs use, then a few more finding them. It was hard, considering I don't speak the language here and had no idea where to start. But I found quite a few and hid them in the fridge, all the way in the back, so they wouldn't go bad.

Now, I realize how stupid it was. "It's dumb, whatever."

"No, it's not! I love them."

Still, I don't look at her.

"Jayden." A hand touches mine. I jump, looking at Jo, afraid of what I'll see. Instead of mocking pity, I see appreciation. It's hidden under hesitancy, but it's still there.

Something warm blooms in my chest.

I clear my throat to get rid of the odd feeling. "Let's eat."

Dinner is good. Delicious, actually. I missed this. Missed Jo's cooking and listening to her and Cole bicker back and forth. The dog lays on my feet the whole time. I try moving my feet from under him, but he keeps moving, laying his furry self on me, panting quickly.

I'm antsy. I see Cole getting excited, and I know he must have something up his sleeve. Sure enough, he returns with a package.

"Just something for you. From both of us."

Jo turns a curious look at me. I feel the blood drain from my face.

Jo opens it, and instantly I recognize the shibari ropes. They're pretty, with multiple ropes in different tones of blue.

I relax. I know this. This is familiar.

Jo laughs. "You gonna tie me up and fuck me silly?"

Cole shrugs, an easy grin on his face. "Sure. But that's not what I got them for."

"Oh yeah?"

Cole glances at me. "Sometimes, the master must become the student."

What is he...oh shit.

Oh shit.

Cole watches me realize what he means, and an evil smile traces across his face. "You're going to use these on Jayden."

42

I snap my gaze over to Jayden. He frowns at the ropes, his eyes flicking from them to Cole to me.

"Excuse me?" he growls.

"You've trussed up Jo plenty of times. It's your turn."

Disbelief fills me. There's no way. Jayden would never agree to that.

There's some sort of silent communication going on between Jayden and Cole. Jayden looks angry, but still, he doesn't say no.

Cole traces my arm with his fingers. "Want to test them out?"

I glance at Jayden. He meets my gaze, his eyes hard.

"I don't think..."

Jayden raises a challenging eyebrow.

Oh fuck. Is this something he'll do? A spark of excitement fills me, and heat blooms between my legs. He would look hot as fuck, all tied up and at my mercy.

"What is it, kitten? Scared?" Jayden mocks, but his body is lined with tension.

"Of course not. Let's do it." I grab the ropes.

"Fuck yeah." Cole stands up behind me.

Once I'm holding them, I realize that I have no idea what I'm doing.

Jayden sees it and smirks.

That does it. I'm doing this regardless.

"Bedroom." Cole bumps me in the direction of the hallway.

The dog eagerly jumps at our feet. Cole laughs and locks the dog away in the bathroom. "So he doesn't eat the food."

Immediately, I feel bad. The dog just got here, and we're locking him away.

"We'll get him in a second." Cole kisses my forehead. "He's had a big day, let him adjust."

Cole moves us to the bedroom. My bedroom.

Fuck. I've never tied a man up before, let alone tried shibari. I don't know what I'm doing. But hell if I'm going to let that stop me.

Jayden stops in front of my bed and then turns to look at me.

"On your back," I order.

Jayden immediately opens his mouth to say something, then snaps it shut. He stands frozen for a second, giving me an angry look, then slowly sits down on the bed.

It's dark enough outside that everything is visible with the lights on in here. He smirks, then lays down stiffly.

Cole runs his hands up and down my arms. "Good girl. Now what?"

I unravel one of the ropes I have in my hands. The bed has four posts. I wonder if I can tie his limbs to them.

I move over to Jayden's right leg. He watches me like a hawk but doesn't move.

My arms hum with energy. This is exciting. He's letting me do this. I grab Jayden's ankle and pull it over to the edge of the bed. I fumble with the rope but tie a knot around his leg, then loop it around the bedpost. I make sure the knot is tight but not too tight.

I smile, then move to the next leg. Once I get that one down, power thrums through me. Jayden's legs are tied pretty securely. He's at my mercy.

I move up to his hands. His big hands. He flexes them, watching me. "Having fun, kitten?"

"Yep." I pop the p, then grab a new roll of rope.

Cole watches. "You gonna teach her something, Jay?"

"Seems like she's doing fine on her own," Jayden growls.

"I want you to teach me a knot," I say.

Jayden looks at me.

My confidence grows. "Teach me how to tie so you can't escape, but it's still safe."

Jayden's gaze is hard, but there's the tiniest bit of softening.

"Here, get that rope." He motions at it. I do as he says. Jayden talks me through a knot, trying to explain how to tie his hand to the post. He gets frustrated when I can't do it exactly right, trying to reach his other hand over to demonstrate. His mobility is slightly limited now that I have his legs.

"Remember. Restrain but don't constrict," he demands.

Finally, I get what I think he's trying to say. I try it again on his other hand and step back, admiring my work. Jayden is stretched out on the bed and completely restrained. I mean, he hasn't tried to get away, but it looks like he's secure.

My pussy throbs unexpectedly. I could do whatever I wanted to him. He's mine—at my mercy.

Jesus, is this what he feels? This could get to my head.

"What are you gonna do, lemon drop? Now's your chance." Cole watches me, a spark in his eyes.

"I..." I glance at Jayden.

"Don't look at him. He already consented to whatever you want to do."

I look at Jayden in surprise. His jaw is hard, and he's glaring at Cole. But when he looks at me, he doesn't say no.

"I don't know when you'll get another chance to do this. Pretty sure he's gonna beat my ass as soon as you let him up. So better take advantage now."

Cautiously, I move to the edge of the bed. The pull of something I've not been allowed to have is so strong. There have been plenty of times I've admired his muscles and tattoos, but he's always been so cold.

I hesitantly pull up Jayden's shirt so I can see his abs. They flex, and his breathing picks up. Fucking hell. They crunch every time he breathes, and they're covered in beautiful, dark tattoos. I glance at Jayden. He watches me with dark eyes.

I run my hand up and down his stomach. Fuck, he's so warm, and his skin is so soft. I catch the goosebumps that run across his skin with my hand.

Oh. He's enjoying this. My pussy gets wet.

"More. You can do more." Cole moves closer.

Jayden stiffens as he does. "Don't fucking touch me," he growls at Cole.

Cole grins bigger. "Touchy."

Jayden moves as if to lunge at Cole, but he's held back by the ropes.

Cole holds his hands up. "I won't touch you. Easy."

Jayden's breathing picks up, and I move down to his slacks. I want to take them off. I want to see if he's hard. Although I can already tell he is. The bulge of his dick presses against his pants. Jayden has a belt on, and I undo it, cussing myself for not taking his clothes off before I tied him up.

"This is ridiculous," Jayden mutters.

Part of me enjoys his embarrassment. This is what he gets for doing the same thing to me for so long.

I inch his pants down, and his dick springs out, tall and heavy and throbbing. My mouth waters. He's so hard for me—for this. He might say he doesn't like it, but part of him does.

I glance at Jayden's dark eyes. Challenge flares in them.

I smirk and grab his cock. Immediately, Jayden stiffens. He pushes up slightly into my grip before relaxing again.

Fuck. I shift, trying to get relief for my aching pussy. Then I stroke Jayden's dick, pulling back on the skin until he bucks up into me again.

"You like that?" I ask.

Jayden says nothing, just yanks on the ropes. I watch as they hold firm.

I grin at him. "What, don't like being under my control?"

Jayden grits his teeth as I pull my hand up and down his shaft. His dick throbs, and I use my other hand to cup his balls. It feels so good to do whatever I want.

Cole moves up behind me. "How can I make you feel good, little one?"

I shift. My pussy is throbbing. Cole immediately sits behind me. "Spread your legs."

I do, and Cole rips my panties. His hot mouth finds my pussy and closes around it. I jerk and moan.

Jayden lets out a grunt as I tighten my hand around his dick. I squeeze harder, jerking him faster. I find Jayden's gaze locked on mine.

I gasp as Cole licks my asshole and flicks his tongue over it. I'm still sensitive from the other night, and I feel the sensation all the way through my stomach.

Jayden smirks. In response, I open my mouth and close it around his cock.

Jayden lets out a real groan as I suck up his length. He bucks his hips up, trying to set the pace, but I don't let him. I go slowly, feeling his thighs tense under my hands.

"Jo..." Jayden warns.

I smirk. What is he gonna do? Nothing. I'm the one in control here.

Cole continues to rim my ass while playing with my clit. He

builds me up quickly, and I realize he's already coaxed an orgasm around the corner. I go to work harder on Jayden's dick, increasing my suction and wrapping my hand around his base.

Pleasure fills me completely. Cole knows how to work my body, and the power I have is already making me buzz. I've never had this power. I've never been in control, and now I have two powerful men at my disposal. And I didn't force the control from them—they gave it to me.

The orgasm rolls over me in waves. I explode, pleasure locking my muscles in powerful pulses. Jayden cusses as I bury his dick in my throat.

When the orgasm starts to fade, Cole immediately comes at me again, playing and licking and sucking and building me up and up and up.

I jerk Jayden off for real now. I go at him hard and aggressively. I watch as he closes his eyes and pushes up into me. His hands open and close like they want to grab me, but they can't. He can't.

"Jo, fuck." Jayden strains.

I'm close. So fucking close. Then Jayden stiffens, and his dick swells. He comes in my mouth, shooting jets of cum that I swallow down eagerly. Mouthful after mouthful. It pushes me over the edge, and I come with him, pulsing against Cole's tongue and fingers.

This orgasm lasts longer than the last and drags out. My head tingles, and I feel...happy, fulfilled, satiated.

I let go of Jayden's dick and immediately move to untie his hands. Cole gets his feet, and when he's done, I move to put the ropes in Cole's pile. As I do, Jayden snatches me up.

I squeal, and Jayden flips me on the bed so I'm under him, and he's on top. He pants, looking down at me. His eyes are sharp, and he growls, "I hope you enjoyed that 'cause that won't happen again for a long, long time."

My hands are pinned under his, and a tingle runs through me

at how helpless I am again. Only this time, I realize it doesn't make me feel helpless.

Jayden smirks, watching me. "You had your fun. Now it's time for my other gift."

"Other..."

Jayden glances at my wrists. "I'm going to tattoo you."

"What?" I look up at him.

He grits his teeth. "Where that other piece of shit touched you. On your wrists."

I clench my jaw. Jayden's domineering tone is back. The one where it doesn't matter what I say.

"I thought you said it was a gift," I snap.

"It is. For me." Jayden closes his eyes for a brief minute, then opens them again. He clears his throat, then backs off me.

I sit up as Jayden sits on the edge of the bed. He tightens his hands into fists, then releases them. "I want to do both wrists. Two skeleton hands holding your wrists. One for me, one for Cole."

I glance at Cole. He doesn't seem surprised.

"I want to..." Jayden struggles for words and runs his hand through his hair. "Fuck."

I sit and wait for him to get the words out.

"I don't want it to cover your scars. I want it to be there for your scars."

I look at him in confusion.

Jayden rubs his face. "Fuck. Words."

It's almost amusing watching him get flustered. Jayden is never flustered. Jayden is a dick, but something has been different about him since we've gotten here. I'm not sure what it is, but it makes me think there's a chance with him.

Slowly, I put my hand out and put it on his arm.

Jayden jumps, then looks over at me. He fixes his intense gaze on me. "I want you to come to me if you feel like cutting. I'll make it hurt for you. But don't do it yourself."

I blink.

Cole sits on the other side of the bed with me. "I've agreed to let Jayden tattoo me when I feel the urge. We're gonna start a piece on my thigh."

Jayden clenches his hands into fists, then gets up and paces in front of us. "I'm going to be there." He gives me a mean glare.

"What Jayden means is he *wants* to be there," Cole says, glaring at Jayden. "If you'll let him."

Jayden pauses stiffly. He battles with himself for a second. "Let me hurt you, Jo."

Cole rubs a hand on my thigh. "Let him make it beautiful."

Jayden runs his hands aggressively through his hair. "You don't have to hide from me anymore, Jo. I'm not perfect, but I'm going to keep working so you never have to hide again. None of us will."

My chest hurts. I want that. I want that more than I'm willing to admit.

"We'll never get bored of you, Jo." Cole leans in. "We're only beginning to crack the surface of Mary Jo Hall, and we're already obsessed. There's nothing that you can say or do that would make us less interested. You've tried. Didn't work." Cole chuckles.

"Stop," I whisper, emotion clogging my throat.

"That word didn't work before, and it won't work now." Cole plants a kiss on my head. "Even if you beg."

I put my hands on both their thighs. They let me sit in silence, collecting my thoughts. Finally, I let out a breath. "I never beg."

JAYDEN

43

One Year Later

I STEP out onto the veranda, and the hot sun immediately beats on my head. Ahead of me, Jo suns herself beside the pool.

We were able to move out of the apartment after only a few months. Jo started another social media account, wearing a mask, and gained popularity making more food content. Cole joined in a lot, and very quickly, Jo reached the popularity she had on her first account. Then, superseded it. I had a lot to say about Jo's choice of sounds and editing styles, and finally, she let me help. At first, I think it was to humor me, then she realized I wasn't half bad at it and let me take over completely. We made enough money doing that to buy a nice house in Mexico and travel, making food vlogs like Jo always wanted to do.

I approach Jo quietly. She has her eyes closed with earbuds in and doesn't notice me. I can't help but admire her tanned skin in the sun. About a month ago, I gave her a rib tattoo with thorny vines crawling up her side, and it looks tantalizing on her. It's healed perfectly, too.

I pluck an earbud out. "What you listening to?"

Jo jumps. "Jesus!"

I laugh. I love seeing her caught off guard.

"Damn it, Jayden." Jo snatches for the earbud, but I keep it from her and hold it up to my ear. "Is this a filthy novel?"

I hear that it is, in fact, a spicy novel.

Jo raises an eyebrow.

I grin at her. I love it when she listens to her nasty books. Cole does, too. She always jumps our bones like we've been starving her of dick.

As I eye fuck her, I notice the seat under Jo is covered in sweat.

"Too hot out here for this shit." I peel my shirt off. "Let's cool off."

Something flashes in Jo's eyes, then it's gone.

"No thanks. Go ahead, though."

I frown at her. Come to think of it, I don't think I've seen Jo in the pool since we got here.

"Nonsense." I reach down and pull her into my arms.

Jo squeals. "My clothes!"

"They'll dry."

"My AirPods!"

"I'll buy you more." I tighten my grip as she scrambles to get away. "Ready?"

"Fuck–"

I jump. We crash into the cold water with a splash. As soon as we're in, I let go of Jo, and she shoots to the surface. I follow lazily behind, grinning as she splashes. Jo kicks to the edge of the pool, then grasps it, heaving for breath.

"See? Feels good." I kick, letting the delicious coolness run over my body.

Jo doesn't answer. Instead, she clings to the wall, her body stiff.

"Jo?"

She stares blankly along the edge of the pool, still heaving for breath.

Something isn't right. Fear shoots through my stomach, and I swim to her. "Jo? You okay?"

I look her over. I can't see anything wrong. I grab her chin and pull her head to look at me.

Jo shudders, blinking back into focus. "Uh..."

I hate the feeling that rushes through me. I feel helpless. Something is wrong with Jo, and I don't know what it is. I squeeze her face, demanding. "Tell me."

"I just...water. Can't do water." Jo pulls herself out of the pool.

I'm confused, and I follow her out of the pool. Jo breathes heavily as if she's just finished running a marathon. "Sorry. It's not usually this bad."

She looks like she can't breathe, and suddenly, I feel horrible.

Oh fuck. I did this. She still can't be around water because of what I did.

A slew of emotions hit me, and at first, all I can feel is anger. Burning, hot anger. I clench my fists and suck in deep breaths. Jo curls up on the lounger again, pulling into as small a ball as she can.

Immediately, my anger is overwhelmed by heartbreaking sadness. I hate seeing Jo upset. I sit down next to her, pulling her into my arms. At first, she fights, but then she relaxes into my grip.

"Jo..." I say. My throat feels clogged.

"I'm fine."

Clearly, she isn't. I want to tell her that I'm sorry. But I know words don't mean anything. Change does.

At least, that's what my therapist tells me. All of us have been going to therapy. It's been online with masks to protect our identity, but we've been going. Jo told us we had to go or she'd leave us. So I planted a tracker in her and made sure she understood she could never leave. But I still went to therapy. It's been the hardest thing

I've ever done in my life. Most sessions, I sweat through my shirt, even though we don't talk about anything meaningful. I've kept the therapist at arm's length. She's nice and all, but she scares me.

Jo tries to shake me off. "I'm fine, Jayden. Really."

I hold her tighter. "I'll make it better, Jo."

"Not your job," she snaps. "Let me up."

"I'll make *me* better," I growl. I hadn't meant to say it, but the moment the words are out, I feel relief.

Jo freezes. Slowly, ever so slowly, she melts back into me. And it's the best feeling in the world.

I rest my chin on the top of her head. I'll make it better. I'm still angry. I'm angry at myself. Angry at the situation. Angry at the world. Although I feel it less, I still feel it, and I hate it.

My therapist says anger is a cover-up emotion. That it's easier to feel angry than it is to feel other things like pain.

Maybe she's onto something.

I shuffle Jo in my arms. I hate it when she's like this. I hate it even more when it's because of me. Maybe it's time I opened up to my therapist.

I'm scared. More scared than I've ever been. But for Jo, maybe I can stop running.

No more hiding. I have to face this. For Jo.

EPILOGUE

FIVE YEARS LATER

ONION POWDER, OR "O.P." for short, jumps at my feet. He's grown from a young dog to an adult but still acts like a puppy. I laugh and push him down. He spins circles around our lavish kitchen, panting with his tongue out. Cole insisted on naming him, and Jayden and I will never stop making fun of him for it.

I put my keys and groceries down on the counter and let out a huge breath. Immediately, I open the ice cream and find a spoon.

Therapy was hard today, but despite that, I've been so much happier since going. It's like a giant weight has been lifted off my shoulders. I feel like a whole different person—less angry, more...found.

"Cookie dough?" Cole moves into the kitchen. "What the fuck? You weren't even going to tell me?" He grabs a spoon and sits next to me at the bar, yanking the carton over to him.

"Fucker," I kick at his legs. "That's mine."

Cole takes a big scoop and wiggles his eyebrows at me. "The last egg has hatched."

"Really?" I jump off the stool and go to the kitchen window, where a bird has made a nest right outside the window. Cole has been obsessed with the progress.

"Did this morning." Jayden walks into the kitchen, wearing a button-down shirt that's unbuttoned at the top, looking relaxed. "Oh sure, don't tell me." He snatches the spoon from Cole. "Hiding the ice cream from me. Lucky I don't off you."

"Pffft. It's been five years since your last one. You couldn't off me if you tried."

I roll my eyes and turn back to the window. There's a muffled yelp.

Sure enough, all the baby birds are curled up and sleeping. The mom must be out getting food. They're so horrendously ugly, but I can't help watching them.

Cole moves to stand beside me. "He took my spoon," he grumbles and grabs my hips, resting his chin on my head.

"Need me to beat him up?"

"Please." We watch the babies for a while. Cole traces his hand up and down my arm. It's covered in tattoos now. Of course, everywhere that their initials aren't. Jayden insisted on keeping those visible. At first, the tattoos started as a release from the pain, but now it's something special that Jayden and I do together. He gets off on marking me; I get off on letting him.

"It's been a month."

"What?" I ask absently.

"A month. Since our reversal."

I freeze.

It has been a month. We didn't need to wait this long, but I told them not to touch me. I thought I was ready, and I've been going to therapy twice a week, but now that there's a real possibility, I'm scared. Terrified, even.

"Jo?" Jayden asks.

I swallow.

Cole turns me around, gripping under my chin and forcing me to look at him. He searches my gaze for a little. "You don't need to be scared."

"I'm not," I lie.

Cole glances back at Jayden, then turns back to me. "Then what is it?"

I close my eyes. "I'm not ready."

But that's it. I am. I feel healed. I don't feel like I'll turn into my mom if I become one. I think Jayden and Cole are ready, too. Cole has worked through some of his past with his mom, and Sam has even visited every once in a while. We've set up a savings account for him, so he'll be set for college. Jayden has also worked through a lot of his trauma. He no longer kills instead of feeling things— shocker—and he's slowly, bit by bit, opening up to himself and us. He and I go swimming every morning now, and he's easier to talk to. I've gotten him hooked on my smutty books.

Recently, I've been watching both men get broody over the baby birds, and despite myself, it makes me swoon. I want to give a child a loving home—one I never grew up in. I think we all do. But still, it's scary. What if I fail? What if *we* fail?

Cole squeezes my cheeks hard enough that it hurts, and I open my eyes. He searches my gaze a while longer. "You know, Jo. I'm not a liar."

I frown. I never said he was.

"And Jayden's not a liar."

"What?" I'm confused now.

Cole smirks. "I said I'd tie you down and fill you with our baby so you could never leave us."

I try to take a step away, but Cole follows me, keeping me pinned to the counter.

"I..."

"Where are you going?"

"I just..."

Jayden's gaze locks on me. He looks hungry. "You'll be ours forever, Jo. This is the one last way we haven't claimed you."

"It's not about claiming!" I keep inching away from Cole, but my pussy is throbbing. He follows slowly, stalking me like a cat.

"True, it's about being a kick-ass parent. But it's *also* about claiming." Cole grins as I back closer to the hallway that leads to the bedrooms. "And you'd look so fucking pretty as ours."

"What about the ice cream? It'll melt."

I reach the end of the counter and back up into the open living room.

"Don't give a fuck about the ice cream."

I cast a desperate glance at O.P., but he only pants, watching us, then looking at the ice cream. Traitor.

Jayden creeps up on my left, cutting off my escape that way. "You got the ropes, Cole?"

"For five years."

"Good." I see the look in Jayden's eyes right before he lunges.

I scream and run, darting to the bedroom. Fear and intoxication fill my lungs. I almost make it to the guest bedroom with the door to the backyard when Jayden snatches me by the hair. He slams me into the hallway wall so hard I cough to catch my breath.

Jayden grins in my face. "You can never hide from us, Jo. Whether you want it or not, we're going to fight you, fuck you, and take care of you." He yanks my hair, causing tears to spring into my eyes. "Just like we always have. Now be our good little girl and fight."

And I do.

THE END

BONUS SCENE

I grip the sides of the sink and close my eyes.

Tired. I'm so incredibly tired. Cole is on baby MJ duty and told me to take a minute to myself. So naturally, I'm hiding in the bathroom. I can still hear her babbled "mama" from here, though.

"She went to the bathroom, baby," Cole coos.

MJ starts crying, and I drop my head down even further. MJ's a momma's girl and has been since she was born a year ago. And I love it. I love the baby cuddles and the hugs and watching all the milestones. But also, I'm fucking exhausted, and it's not even 9 AM.

The front door rings, and I stand up. Who's here? Straightening my hair, I walk out.

"Baby!" Our neighbor Rosa walks in and throws her hands in the air. O.P. jumps up and down at her feet, barking. Rosa has been our neighbor for years. She started dogsitting O.P. when we needed, and she spoiled him rotten. He always gains weight when we're gone. I swear she's feeding him ice cream.

Rosa bustles into the living room, putting down her backpack and sitting down next to Cole and MJ. When MJ sees her, she smiles from ear to ear.

"Thanks for coming." Cole smiles as MJ crawls over to Rosa.

I don't remember inviting her.

Jayden walks into the room, wearing a nice pair of jeans and a button-down. I frown. What's going on?

Cole stands, patting his pockets down. "Got everything you need?"

"You know I do, honey. Now get."

"What's going on?" I ask as Cole walks past me. He winks. "We're going out for the weekend."

"What?"

Jayden wraps me in a hug from behind and whispers in my ear, "Surprise."

I turn to look at him. Jayden smiles gently down at me. "Rosa is gonna take care of things here."

I've never left MJ before. My stomach clenches.

Jayden whispers lower, "There are cameras up in every room. We can watch everything the whole time."

I watch my happy baby girl wobble on Rosa's lap. Then she spots me, and her smile widens.

"Ready?" Cole smacks my ass.

Jayden starts dragging me toward the front door. I dig my feet in. "No, wait. Where are we going?"

"Go on, honey. We'll be fine." Rosa helps MJ walk along the back of the couch. "You know she loves to play with me."

Jayden hands me off to Cole, who whisks me outside. Panic fills me. "Wait!"

"You need a break, Jo."

I don't want to leave my baby. What about her feeding schedule? And nap times? And what about when she cries?

"Jo." Cole grabs my face and forces me to look at him. His voice gets soft. "Rosa knows MJ. She's raised five kids of her own. I'd never leave our baby with her if I didn't think she'd take care of her."

Jayden brushes past us. "I told her I'd kill her if she let anything happen. So there's that."

"Jayden!" I gasp.

He shrugs. "It's the truth."

Cole lets go of my face but continues to look earnestly into my eyes. "You're a wonderful momma, Jo. But you haven't taken a day off in a year. We have a whole weekend away, if you'll let us."

My first reaction is no. I can't leave my baby. But I do want time off.

"You *can* leave her," Cole says softly. He fishes in his pocket and grabs his phone, pulling up a screen with camera footage. I see Rosa and MJ playing on the floor. Safe.

I let out a huge breath. Maybe this will be good.

"Good girl." Cole grins and swoops me up. "Now, let's go."

"Cole," I laugh as he shoves me in the back of Jayden's truck. He follows me in with an evil smile. "Been a while since I've feasted on you."

"Not while we're driving." Jayden gets in and pulls off. "Strap her in, fucker."

Cole grumbles, then leans over to me. "Safety first, princess."

We drive for an hour while Cole rambles stories about when he and Jayden were kids. Most of the stories involve something embarrassing Jayden did. I know Cole's trying to distract me, and I appreciate it. I keep glancing at the phone monitor, which also gives me peace. After about an hour, Jayden reaches into the front seat and tosses something back. "Put this on."

I blink as it lands on my thigh. It's a black piece of fabric. Cole snatches it up. "Blindfold time."

"Wait, no–" I protest, but Cole wraps the blindfold around my head.

"Say no again; it gets me hot."

Cole's heavy hands land on mine, pinning them to my lap so I can't mess with it. Excitement thrums through my veins. "What are you doing?"

"Nothing you won't like." Cole squeezes my hands.

I feel the truck roll to a stop, and then Cole's door pops open. Hot air rushes in, and immediately, I notice it smells fresh. Cole helps me scoot to the edge of the seat, then grabs me and carries me over his shoulder.

"Put me down," I giggle.

"You hear something, Jay?"

I raise my hand to try and peek out of my blindfold. Someone swats it back down, then Jayden says, "Nope, didn't hear shit."

I'm carried for a bit, and then it sounds like we are walking up some steps. I hear the birds and the frogs, but other than that, there's nothing.

A door opens.

"Ready, lemon drop?"

Cole sets me down. Immediately, I reach up to take the blindfold off. Where the hell are we?

Warm hands help me pull it off, and instantly, I'm greeted with the sight of a living room with exposed wooden beams. The kitchen is on the right, there's a spiral staircase to the left, and bear and moose decor.

I stand frozen. It's...the cabin. The cabin they first took me to.

I blink. No, it's not the cabin. Things are different. All the windows are open, and warm air floods gently in. The bears and moose on the decor have traditional Mexican clothing stitched onto them. In addition, the kitchen is much more advanced. The most recent amenities are set up, and there's a wooden sign that says 'Lemon Drop's kitchen.'

Emotion fills me. I pull in a breath and turn.

Both men are looking at me with soft expressions.

"What? How?"

"You like it?" Cole grins.

Nostalgia hits me. I turn back around and look at it all again. The space is so homey, warm, and welcoming. A smile moves across my face. Despite everything, I've missed this place.

I turn back to the men. "You built this?"

Cole smiles. "Missed it too much. Loved the things we did here." In an instant, a predatory look sweeps over his face. He watches me intensely.

It makes me freeze. I glance at Jayden. He also looks at me like I'm a piece of steak and he hasn't eaten in weeks. I haven't seen them look like this in a long time. They've both been in dad mode for so long, but this? This is exactly what they used to look like. Mean and hungry.

The front door is still open, and Cole shuts it slowly while watching me. He slowly flicks the lock over. "You want to explore?"

I swallow. Cole's pupils are blown. Jayden's are, too, and he watches me with utter focus.

"What are you doing?"

Cole smirks but doesn't answer.

I take a step back toward the living room. Both men cock their heads. The air is charged with energy.

I take another step back, my muscles coiled tight.

Cole smirks. "Better run, little one."

Jayden lifts an eyebrow. "Better hide, kitten. You won't like it when we catch you."

And I do. I turn and whirl, darting toward the spiral steps. Flying up them two at a time, I launch myself into the loft. It looks just like the other one did, with a huge bed taking up most of the space and a balcony looking out to the living room.

Heavy footsteps follow me.

I dart to the wardrobe and yank it open, hoping to find something to defend myself. It's full of...sex toys? I snatch up a whip and whirl. Both men have made it to the top and fan out. Jayden goes to the other side of the bed, and Cole heads for me.

"Caught you." Cole grins. "You know, you're shit at hiding."

I lash the whip out at Cole, and he jumps back in surprise. It's enough to give me an opening, and I rush past him. I dart to the railing, ready to jump to the couch below, but Jayden snatches me up by my waist and growls. "What did I fucking tell you?"

He throws me back onto the bed. "You don't get to fucking hurt yourself." His face is alive with anger.

I scramble to my knees. "I wasn't trying –"

Cole snatches the whip off the bed. "No more of that. I think we should punish her, Jay."

"Agreed." Jayden is on top of me in an instant, flipping me over and pinning my face to the bed. "Disobedient girl."

I struggle, their dominance running straight to my pussy.

"Submit, nasty thing."

"Never." I wriggle under Jayden's harsh hold, but it only serves to push my ass up in the air more. Hands grab my leggings and rip them down my legs.

"Fight harder, babe. You can get away." Cole croons.

Jayden lets up on the pressure, and I whirl, scrambling to get up. Cole is right there, and I swing at him.

My arm is caught, and Jayden hauls me up into his lap. He's already naked and chuckles. "No claws to the face. You know Cole is weird about his skin."

"Fuck you," I'm heaving for breath, but exhilaration runs through me. I feel alive. My blood is burning.

"You've done it now." Jayden shifts and pulls me up on him. "Cole, lube."

Cole tosses it at Jayden, and he catches it with one hand. I try to scramble away from the arm still holding me, but Jayden has me wrapped tight. He fists his dick. "C'mon, kitten. That the best you got?"

"Fuck you, you fucking prick."

He chuckles. "That's more like it. Now relax for me."

Jayden yanks me back onto his lap, his hard dick between my cheeks. Effortlessly, he lifts me up enough to situate his dick to my ass.

"No." I struggle, adrenaline running through me.

"Fight me, and I'll make it hurt."

I fight him.

Jayden shoves me down on his dick, his cock splitting my ass open. I scream, overwhelmed by a rush of pain.

"Shhhh. You asked for this." Jayden holds me still. He's only partially seated in me, but the stretch is everything. It's been so long since we've messed around like this.

"You look so pretty when you fight." Cole grabs my chin and cheeks and forces my face up to him. He leans in to lick a tear that has traced down my face. He groans a deep, heady sound. Cole strokes his dick, leaning into me. "Keep going, Jo. I want to feel you struggle as I fuck you."

I groan. The pain in my ass is slowly turning to pleasure as Jayden pumps into me slowly. Jayden lays us back down so he's on his back, and I'm laying on my back on top of him. Cole gets on top of us and lines his dick up with my entrance. I kick back against Cole, and he only grins, slowly pushing into me. The fullness immediately stretches me, and I groan.

"That's it. Let us know how much we're hurting you." Cole throws his head back. Once he's fully seated in me, he reaches down and grabs one of my nipples.

The sensation feels amazing. My breasts have been so much more sensitive since having a kid, and Cole knows that. He rolls my nipple between his fingers, causing pleasure to shoot through my body. I arch my back.

Both men begin to pound into me, finding a rhythm and

fucking me steadily. Their dicks rub against spots that make me see stars. It hurts, which only adds to the sensations.

"You're such a sexy momma." Cole groans, pushing gently into me. "This is everything that I've ever wanted. Having you, having our family."

"Cole," I groan and struggle to get my arm free. Jayden lets it go, and I reach up, scraping my nails down his chest.

"Yes?"

"Stop. Being. Gentle." I rip my nails into his skin.

Cole laughs, slamming his dick into me. It causes a burst of pain that rushes through me. My nipples harden as pleasure builds.

Both men start slamming into me harder, rutting into me and chasing their own pleasure. My body bounces, and my pussy clenches around them.

"Jo. Our pretty little slut."

"Gorgeous whore."

I moan. My orgasm builds.

"Gonna come for us, lemon drop?"

I arch my back, chasing the pleasure. Cole shifts so his dick hits my G-spot, and my orgasm slams into me. Blinding pleasure explodes within me, and I squeeze my eyes shut.

"Good girl," Cole groans.

Pleasure washes over me in waves.

"Eyes," Cole growls.

Instantly, I snap my eyes open.

"Fuck," Cole watches me and picks up his pace, pounding into me. Beneath me, Jayden pulses and stiffens. He groans my name as he comes.

That pushes Cole over the edge, and he also comes inside me. He moans, pushing deeply into me.

As my orgasm fades, the boys pull out of me. Jayden strokes my hair back, and Cole jumps up. He comes back with towels and cleans me up. I'm still lying there, my muscles liquid. I feel warm and relaxed.

Once we're clean, Cole settles in next to me. He runs his fingers down my arms, making goosebumps run up and down my arms.

"How did we get so lucky, Jay?"

Jayden traces up and down my other arm. "We committed a felony?"

I scoff. "One felony?"

Jayden chuckles and pinches me. "Careful. I'm ready to fuck you again."

I roll my eyes and stare at the ceiling. The sound of birds fills the cabin, and I suck in a breath. I didn't know how much I missed this place. It's fucked up. I shouldn't miss it at all. But I do.

"Whew. That was a great first round." Cole swings his feet over the bed. "You all relax. I'm gonna make some food."

"Cole," I groan. He's learned so much since helping me in the kitchen, but that's usually my job.

"I won't hear it." He bounds down the stairs. I hear clattering, and suddenly, I want to get up. To explore the cabin. To bask in old memories and see what they've stocked the kitchen with.

I pad through the property. It's almost an exact replica of the old cabin, minus the handcuffs in the guest bedroom and the shitty baseball posters in the basement. Although this cabin feels...lighter. More free.

When I wander into the kitchen, Cole is flipping pancakes. Jayden's there, too. He spots me, then nods at the freezer. "Got you something."

I freeze.

He just chuckles. "A good something."

I roll my eyes. "It better not be a dildo."

Cole looks genuinely offended for a second. "Why would you need a dildo? You have us."

I pop open the freezer. It's fully stocked with my chicken and sage meals. I suck in a breath. I've missed them. They don't sell that brand down here in Mexico, and just seeing them makes me nostalgic.

Jayden gives me a soft smile.

I shake my head. How did I go from them kidnapping me to spoiling me? I sit down at the table. "So. What's the plan this weekend?"

"Fuck you senseless. Give you more tattoos. Enjoy the peace." Jayden leans back in his chair.

I laugh. "Where else are you going to tattoo? You've already given me so many."

Jayden eyes me. "I can think of some blank spaces."

Instantly, I cross my arms. "No. You will not be tattooing my pussy."

Jayden just shrugs.

"Jayden," I growl. For a second, I worry that he'll do it regardless of what I say. But since he's been in therapy, he's been really good at learning my hard limits and not pushing them unless I ask him to.

Jayden rolls his eyes at me, but his look is soft.

I let out a huge breath. The boys have grown so much since everything. And I love it. They're a perfect mix of asshole and attentive.

I also lean back in my chair and pull in a deep breath. Despite my initial reservations about leaving today, this is nice. I don't have to be responsible for anyone else. Or cook. Or do anything, really. It's nice.

"Food's ready." Cole plops a plate of steaming hot pancakes in front of me. Ironically, I'm sitting in the same spot I was when they fed me pancakes last time. I lift an eyebrow. "Are these drugged?"

Cole laughs. "Maybe."

I turn to him. I don't like that evasive answer.

He grins at me. "Eat up, lemon drop."

"What did you put in them?"

Cole shrugs. "Little this, little that."

"Cole," I growl.

"Listen." He leans in. "You deserve a break. A chance to let go. We're offering that to you. If I were you, I'd take it."

My mind turns a mile a minute. "Who will check on MJ?"

"Us. We'd never leave her without access to at least one of us."

I glance at the food. All the things that could go wrong rush across my head.

"Trust, Jo. Remember, we're learning trust."

I look up at Jayden. He raises a dark eyebrow.

"No more running. No more hiding. Just let go and trust us." Cole kisses the top of my head. "You can do that, yeah?"

I let out a breath. Over the past few years, the men have consistently shown effort to be there for me, even when it's hard for them. Especially once MJ showed up. They work tirelessly to support her and me. If there was ever a time for trust, it'd be now.

Before I can overthink it, I grab a fork and take a bite of the food. It's heavenly. The pancakes are pillowy and soft. Cole has added bacon, too, and I enjoy the salty side.

The men watch me eat, pupils blown again. I slow down, muttering, "You've seen me eat before, chill."

"Sassy, even while drugged." Cole shakes his head and laughs.

I don't feel any different. But as soon as my plate is cleared, I feel a rush of lightheadedness. I blink to clear it.

"There it is." Cole comes up behind me and grabs me. "Fall into me, Jo. Let go and fall. Let me show you how good trust can be."

The End.

ACKNOWLEDGMENTS

If you don't already, stalk me on social media. I love meeting new people and I love being stalked. Go figure.

Tiktok: alina_may_author

Instagram: alina_may_author

Facebook: Alina May's Book Babes

Fun fact: I never planned on writing a book to this duet. When the emotions of the characters got involved, I got scared and ran for the hills. The end, over, done, bye! But thanks to the gentle bullying of my readers and insistence by Jayden, Cole, and Jo themselves, this baby was born. So my first thank you is to my readers for helping these character's voices be heard.

Secondly, thank you to my amazing beta readers, Sarah, Amanda, Alex, and Laurelyn. Ya'll keep it real and you crack me the fuck up. Thanks for the amazing ideas, edits, and lines.

And as always, thank you to my amazing editor, Taylor. You call me on my bullshit and somehow make it look like I know how to spell. A miracle worker, and an amazing friend. Love ya.